KU-100-418

**Books should be returned on or before the
last date stamped below.**

To ... on
a ... e
Sc ... w
bu ... e
ba ... n
yo ... g.
To ... e
sc

An ... h
lac ... e
sc ... a
Qu ... e
Ac ... al
the

# TOPAZ STEALS
# THE SHOW

Helen Bailey

*Illustrated by Bill Dare*

First published in Great Britain by
Hodder Children's Books 2005
This Large Print edition published by
BBC Audiobooks by arrangement with
Hodder Children's Books 2007

ISBN: 978 1405 661508

**British Library Cataloguing in Publication Data available**

Printed and bound in Great Britain by
Antony Rowe Ltd., Chippenham, Wiltshire

*For Karen Halstead.*

*Greatly loved. Sorely missed.*

# Chapter One

Barely had a voice finished announcing, 'Welcome to Precious Gems Stage School. The auditions are about to begin!' than there was a loud roar and a crowd of girls wearing Lurex, Lycra and legwarmers began stampeding towards the door of the school theatre.

Topaz clung nervously to the wall. Girls who, moments before, had been sweetly singing scales or gracefully practising dance moves pushed, shoved and clawed their way to the front of the queue, their faces set with steely determination. An audition for stage school was one step closer to becoming a star and *nothing* and *no one* was going to get in the way of their ambition.

Topaz felt a sharp elbow in her side.

'Move!' ordered a blonde girl, stamping on Topaz's toes as she swept past.

Topaz tried to move, but collided with a large woman with peroxide-blonde hair and a shiny purple tracksuit. The woman paused for a split second, glared at Topaz and pushed her out of the way, sending Topaz crashing into a nearby chair before marching down the corridor screeching, 'Octavia! Keep going, sweetie, Mummy's right behind you!'

*Is this what it would be like at stage school?* Topaz wondered as she picked herself up and watched the pushy blonde's head bob up and down as she elbowed her way through the crowd. *One long fight to be noticed amongst a crowd of catty girls and their pushy mothers?*

Her trampled toes throbbed and her leg hurt from where she'd hit the chair, and for a moment she felt completely overwhelmed. Everyone seemed so confident, so polished, so talented. She looked down at her plain black trousers and white T-shirt. She didn't even look the part! 'Normal everyday clothes' the letter had said. What sort of girls wore feathers and sequinned dresses as everyday clothes?

From the moment Topaz had opened her fish and chips, wrapped in an old copy of *The Starbridge Gazette*, and seen the article about Precious Gems Stage School, she'd been determined to win a place and become a star. But now, waiting for the auditions to begin, she felt lost and lonely and *very* out of place.

The crowd seemed to have stopped surging forward. At the far end of the corridor the doors to the theatre opened and a woman's voice called out, 'Ladies and gentlemen! There's no need to rush!'

The crowd immediately fell silent. Topaz craned her neck to try and see who was speaking, but she was too far back. What little view she had was obscured by a girl who had so many feathers in her hair it looked as if a peacock had landed on her head.

The voice boomed out again. 'Take a look at the number you have been given and listen carefully. You'll be asked to come into the theatre in groups of three.'

Topaz stood on tiptoe to try and get a look at who was speaking but only managed to get feathers up her nose, causing her to sneeze.

Feather Girl turned round and gave Topaz a dirty look. No one wanted to miss their number being called out.

'Group One!' the voice announced.

Topaz looked at her piece of paper. She'd been holding it so tightly it was now a damp crumpled ball. Group One! Thank goodness she was in the first group. If she had to wait any longer she might explode.

As Topaz began to push through the crowd towards the school theatre, a high-pitched voice rang out.

'You don't seem to understand!' the voice screeched. 'My daughter Octavia Quaver *has* to have an early audition. She *can't* be in Group Ten. She has a recording for a Slurp 'n' Burp fizzy drinks commercial in an hour.'

As Topaz reached the front of the queue she saw the large woman who had pushed her over, jabbing her finger at a woman Topaz recognized as the Headmistress of the school, Miss Adelaide Diamond.

Miss Diamond said something out of earshot and Purple Tracksuit exploded again.

'I'm not taking the word "no" from a past-it-over-the hill-has-been!'

Topaz's mouth dropped open in astonishment. It was true that Miss Diamond no longer acted, but before opening the stage school she had been a major star.

'What a *dreadful* woman,' Topaz said

5

to a girl standing next to her. 'Who *does* she think she is, talking to Miss Diamond like that?'

She turned to look at the girl and realized, too late, it was the blonde who had elbowed her in the back and stamped on her toes.

The girl glared at Topaz. 'That,' she said with a sneer, 'is my mother. *I'm* Octavia Quaver.'

There was something about Octavia that made Topaz glad she'd been rude about her mother. She looked like a brittle stick of pink and white rock. On her feet were white tap-shoes and her blonde curls were swept back by a thick white hair band, but from her legwarmers to her leotard she was dressed in shiny, sugary-pink Lycra.

Octavia saw Topaz's number. 'Give me that. You can go in at the end. After all,' she sneered, looking Topaz up and down, 'it's not as if you're likely to have another audition to go to.'

'Get lost!' muttered Topaz under her breath.

The door to the theatre swung open and a voice called out, 'Group One!'

In a flash, Octavia Quaver grabbed the numbered piece of paper out of Topaz's hand and darted towards the theatre doors, tossing her own number back over her shoulder. Topaz gave chase, but moments after Octavia slipped inside the theatre, the doors slammed shut.

\*     \*     \*

Topaz seethed with anger at the way Octavia had double-crossed her. She pleaded with the lady on the door to let her in. She thought about standing in the corridor and screaming rude words at Octavia to ruin her audition. She almost cried with frustration. But still she couldn't get in. There was nothing for it but to wait her turn.

*You'll get what you deserve one day*, thought Topaz as, twenty minutes later, the doors swung open and Octavia swept past wearing a sweatshirt saying 'No Angel' in rhinestones across the back—whilst her mother trotted after her shrieking, 'Another great performance, darling!

7

Well done!'

*      *      *

The groups were called out one by one until finally there were only a few people left waiting. Topaz's bottom was numb from sitting for hours on the hard chairs lining the corridor. Every time she shifted in the seat another part of her anatomy either became numb, or worse, fizzed with pins and needles. She was sure those around her must think she had ants in her pants the way she kept fidgeting. Eventually, a weary voice called out, 'Group Ten!' and, with wobbly legs, she walked into the school theatre.

The first thing Topaz noticed when she entered the hall wasn't the usual rich and inviting smell of the theatre, but the pong of stinky stale school dinners and dust.

The Precious Gems school hall had to accommodate assemblies and school meals as well as performances and concerts, so it was a strange mix of traditional theatre and standard school

8

hall. The walls were draped with shiny blue material in an attempt to disguise the gym equipment stored behind them. Thick crimson velvet curtains held back by gold rope framed the small stage. A bright spotlight picked out a girl with red hair and glasses, playing the piano. Below the stage was a small orchestra pit in front of which stood row upon row of thin wooden chairs.

Slipping in at the back next to a blonde girl, Topaz sat on one of the chairs and then sat on her hands to stop them shaking.

She shot a sideways glance at the girl. Straight hair. The sort of hair that could be flicked casually over one shoulder and still stay perfect. Topaz was sure she recognized her but couldn't think from where.

The blonde noticed her looking and

smiled. 'She's good,' she whispered, nodding towards the stage where the girl was coming towards the end of her piano audition.

Topaz wasn't interested in the piano player, but closer inspection of the blonde made her seem even more familiar.

'I'm sure I've seen you before,' Topaz whispered back. 'Were you in the after-school stage club at Starbridge Middle?'

The girl ran her hands through her hair and shook her head. 'No. I've been to school all over the place but my father thought it was time for me to go to stage school.' Her voice was friendly but she sounded bored. 'I didn't need to come to the auditions but I insisted on it.'

Topaz was about to ask her what she meant when there was a yell, a crash and a high-pitched scream as the pianist fell off the edge whilst leaving the stage and landed with a huge thud in the orchestra pit. Sheet music fluttered down on to the people sitting in the front row.

'Sapphire Stratton!' called a voice as the blonde moved past Topaz and glided towards the stage.

Topaz groaned inwardly and put her head in her hands. No wonder she recognized her! Sapphire Stratton! Vanessa and Sinclair Stratton's daughter! All her family were in show business. She'd practically been born with a theatre programme in her mouth. Why on earth would someone like Sapphire go to an after-school stage club?

*I'm such a dork*, she thought. *A total utter dork.*

\*     \*     \*

Topaz sat dejectedly at the back of the hall. Other than the teachers at the front, it was now empty.

She'd been dreaming of this chance for so long, but she'd been foolish to think she could get into stage school. One minor part in the after-school stage club play was all the experience she had. She couldn't play the piano like the red-haired girl and wasn't part of the acting aristocracy like Sapphire Stratton. Even when the letter had arrived offering her an audition she'd had to pinch herself. She'd thought someone might have made it up to punish her for forging her mum's signature on the entrance form. What hope did a girl from a tiny top-floor flat in Andromeda Road have of becoming a star?

*What a fool I've been*, she thought miserably. *I'll have nothing to show for an afternoon except a numb bum.*

'Next!'

Topaz looked around and realized that 'Next' had to mean her. She hurried to the front of the hall and clambered up the steps on to the stage. Dust swirled and floated through the beams of light and she had to blink several times before she could focus her eyes. But the instant she stood in the spotlight, her nerves left her. At that moment she knew, beyond any doubt, that more than *anything* in the world, she wanted to be a star.

*This is where I belong!* she thought to herself. *This is it! This is where I am meant to be!*

All she had to do now was convince the school that she should be offered a place.

*          *          *

In the front row of the school hall, with a teacher on either side of her, sat Miss Adelaide Diamond, Head mistress of Precious Gems Stage School, looking at the names she had ticked off her list. There was only one left.

'Octavia Quaver?' Miss Diamond asked.

'No!' said Topaz indignantly. 'She stole my number so she could get in first. I'm Topaz Love, but I'd like to be known as Topaz L'Amour. I think it sounds better. Don't all stars change their names?'

Adelaide Diamond was too tired to argue. It had been a long day and there were only so many renditions of *Tomorrow* that a person could stand.

On her list she crossed out two entries. One was Topaz's surname.

Next to that she wrote, 'L'Amour'. Then, with more force than was necessary, she crossed out 'Octavia Quaver'.

*     *     *

To the left of Miss Diamond, a small man wearing a grey polo-neck jumper was doodling in a notebook with pink pages.

Without looking up he demanded in a clipped voice, 'Speciality?'

Topaz looked blank.

The man sighed loudly, as if even breathing was too much effort. 'Singing? Acting? Dancing?'

'Oh! I see!' said Topaz. 'Yes. Sorry. Yes. I do all three.'

The woman on the right of Miss Diamond spoke up. She was as thin as a pipe-cleaner and everything about her was angular: from the shape of her head, clearly outlined by her very short hair, to her glasses, worn on a

14

chain around her narrow neck.

'All three?' the Pipe-cleaner squeaked, pursing her lips. 'Next you will tell us that you also play a musical instrument.'

Topaz gave the Pipe-cleaner her most dazzling smile. 'I can play chopsticks on the recorder,' she said.

Pipe-cleaner and Polo-neck hid their faces behind their notebooks. Topaz could see they were laughing, but it didn't matter. It was better to be laughed at than ignored.

The Headmistress held up her hand to silence her sniggering staff and asked Topaz to begin her audition pieces.

\*        \*        \*

Adelaide Diamond knew there were other entrants far more suitable than the girl now performing her heart out.

The red-haired girl, Ruby Ruddle, was immensely talented. It was unfortunate that she suffered from stage fright and had fallen into the orchestra pit at the end, but her

15

injuries would heal and they could work on her nerves.

Sapphire Stratton had given a very polished and assured presentation and had superb technique, but lacked any sparkle. She'd asked to do an audition along with everyone else, but there'd been no need. There was an open place for her at Precious Gems, because it would be a huge coup for the school to teach a young Stratton. Unfortunately, she didn't appear to have any hunger or passion for the business. Perhaps it was because success for a Stratton was almost guaranteed.

Miss Diamond studied Topaz with interest. The girl was unremarkable-looking, of average height, average build and neither pretty nor plain, but there was something fresh and determined about her that made Miss Diamond sit up and take notice. She didn't sing particularly well, and her dance routine was so enthusiastic her legs resembled an out-of-control baby giraffe, whilst her arms spun like windmills in a gale. There was more determination and enthusiasm than experience, and yet, and yet . . .

Adelaide Diamond leaned forward in her seat. The rows of amber beads around her neck swung, bounced off her ample bosom and then clacked together as if giving a round of applause.

'Thank you, Topaz!' shouted Miss Diamond. 'We'll let you know!'

Topaz had been about to burst into another song-and-dance routine. She'd enjoyed being the centre of attention.

'When?' she asked.

'When we've finished the auditions,' said the Pipe-cleaner in a stiff voice. 'They go on for several weeks.'

Topaz was reluctant to leave the stage. She felt so at home in the spotlight. Even more than she did in her own home. Now she was going to have to wait weeks to hear if she would be offered a place.

'I just don't know how I am going to *live* not knowing!' she said.

'I think you'll manage,' said Miss Diamond, trying to stifle a smile, whilst on her left and right side both teachers sat stony-faced.

*　　　*　　　*

Once Topaz had left the hall, Miss Diamond turned to her right.

'Gloria, do we know whether the girl has applied for Rhapsody's Theatre Academy?'

Gloria, the bespectacled Pipe-cleaner, shrugged her bony shoulders. 'She's got no technique,' she said through tight lips.

'Anton?' Adelaide Diamond asked to her left.

Polo-neck raised his hands and rolled his eyes. 'And absolutely no stage experience or discipline! Those audition pieces were obviously put together in her bedroom.'

Miss Diamond nodded, stiffly pulled herself out of her seat and began to leave the hall. Anton Graphite, Artistic Director, and Gloria Gold, Director of Music, sank down in their seats with relief. Thank goodness! For one dreadful moment they had thought the Topaz girl was going to be offered a place. They'd rarely seen the Headmistress look so interested in someone so obviously without training or experience.

'It's all very well, Glo,' hissed Anton, 'but it would have been us who would have been asked to make a silk purse out of a sow's ear.'

Gloria pursed her lips and sucked air in between her teeth. 'You're so right, Anton,' she murmured. 'So right.'

\*      \*      \*

At the door of the hall, Adelaide Diamond turned back. The spotlight still lit the stage, but somehow, without that girl there, it seemed a little dimmer.

'Get a letter out tonight offering Topaz L'Amour a scholarship,' she called back to her horrified colleagues. 'I don't want her slipping through the net.'

19

# Chapter Two

The day the letter arrived, offering Topaz a scholarship at Precious Gems Stage School, was the happiest day of her life. She immediately started to plan her career as a star.

She spent hours after school practising singing into a hairbrush in front of a mirror.

Dancing was more complicated. The lack of a full-length mirror made working out dance moves difficult. She tried to prop up a mirror on the bedroom floor, but all she could see were her knees, so she resorted to waiting until after dark and dancing in front of the bedroom window with the light on. There was a great reflection, and if anyone was standing at the bus stop on the other side of Andromeda Road, they were her audience. Sometimes they would wave at her and she would wave back—though once a group of boys didn't so much wave as, well, it didn't matter.

Tap-dancing in the bathroom was less successful. She pushed drawing-pins into the heel and toe of her trainers, and practised making tap-dancing sounds. There wasn't actually room to move in the bathroom, so she ended up jumping up and down on the spot, clacking away until the people in the flat below began banging on the ceiling. In revenge, Topaz started flushing the toilet continuously for half an hour at four-thirty every afternoon. She knew that was the time her

21

downstairs neighbours liked to watch the cookery game show, *Proof of the Pudding.* If she flushed the loo it caused the water pipes running through their living room to clank noisily together. They might bang on the floor because of her drawing-pin tap-dancing, but they'd be too embarrassed to ask her to stop flushing the toilet.

*     *     *

During lessons at Starbridge Middle she practised signing her autograph.

At first she decided that a nice touch would be to make the 'o' in L'Amour a heart, and scribbled 'Topaz L'Am♥ur' wherever and whenever she could. But if she became famous, would she have *time* to write 'Topaz L'Am♥ur' for all the fans pushing pen and paper her way? Probably not. Perhaps a sort of scrawl would be better? She'd seen pictures of autographs in magazines and most bore no resemblance to a name, just a mark, as if a heavy book had been dropped on a passing spider.

On the other hand, if she got *really* famous, she'd need some postcards printed with her autograph *and* her picture, which she could just hand out. Maybe, next time she was in town, it wouldn't do any harm just to pop in to the print shop and see how much it would cost.

Then there was the matter of preparing a speech to accept one of the several Golden Nugget Awards that were destined to come her way. In her head she could already imagine sweeping down the red carpet in a dress by the hottest designer of the moment: 'Topaz, it would be an *honour* to dress you. Here are twenty outfits to choose from. Keep them all!'

The audience would be on their feet giving her a standing ovation, just trying to touch her as she made her way to thc podium.

She'd wipe away a tear with a perfectly manicured hand, clutch the Golden Nugget and say, 'This is a *total* shock. I had *no* idea. I've *nothing* prepared,' before giving a word-perfect, ten-minute speech.

Thinking about what to say for the rest of the speech had proved rather difficult.

Most stars said, 'I'd like to thank my family for their unfailing support and encouragement and for always believing in me.' Or something like that.

The only family Topaz had was her mum, and when the letter from Precious Gems had arrived, her mum had collapsed at the kitchen table, buried her face in her hands and sobbed.

'I'm sorry I forged your signature on the form,' Topaz said, shocked to see her mum in tears. 'I never really thought I would even get an audition.'

Topaz's mum continued to weep. Topaz had never seen her so upset.

'Is it that I changed my name without asking you?' Tears began to roll down Topaz's face. 'I'm sorry. I just thought it sounded better if I'm going to be a star.'

'A life in show business is so hard,' said her mother, wiping her eyes with a tea towel. 'I just don't want to see you hurt, like I was.'

Lola Love stood up from the table and began to clear away the breakfast things. She'd said more than she meant to. One day, she'd tell Topaz everything. That she hadn't always been a cleaner. That she too had once been on the stage and had dreams of stardom.

'Mum?' said Topaz. 'What do you mean, like you? Did *you* once want to be a star?'

Topaz knew from the look on her mother's tear-stained face that the subject was closed and she wouldn't get an answer. It was the same look she gave whenever Topaz asked questions about her father. It was a look which said, 'Just don't go there.'

\*     \*     \*

With the thought of starting at Precious Gems only a few weeks away, the summer holidays should have been perfect, but they turned out to be long and lonely.

When Topaz told her best friend,

Janice Stone, that she had a place at Precious Gems, Janice seemed genuinely delighted.

'That's great!' she said. 'Will you still talk to me when you're famous?'

'Of course I will,' said Topaz. 'I'll make sure you get the best tickets for all my shows.'

But when they streamed out of the gates of Starbridge Middle for the last time at the end of the summer term, shouting at each other, 'See you at the High!' Janice wandered off with Kylie Slate, whom she supposedly detested.

A couple of days into the holidays, Topaz sent Janice a text message saying, 'CU?' and Janice texted back, 'NT2Day' but when Topaz was in the newsagent's trying to read *Snapped!* celebrity magazine before the sulky assistant said, 'Are you going to buy that or just look at the pictures?' which was the whole point of the magazine, she saw Janice and Kylie go past the shop, *arm in arm*, giggling! Janice saw her and was about to wave, but Kylie pulled her away and shot Topaz a look which said, 'She's mine now.'

That was the last Topaz saw of Janice all summer. She sent a couple more text messages, but nothing came back. Usually, within moments of sending a message, she'd get one back. Janice had very fast texting fingers. But after several days of checking that her phone was switched on and the battery was working, there was still no text from Janice.

She sent Janice one last message asking her to keep in touch, but as she pressed the 'Send' button and saw 'KIT' drift off to wherever messages went to before they were delivered, she knew she wouldn't get a reply.

\*       \*       \*

On the morning of the third day of the

school holidays, a letter arrived with the school uniform list. It ran to several pages and sent her mum into a manic mental meltdown. 'How ever are we going to afford it all?'

The list read:

## Skirt
Pleated. Dove grey, no extremes of length.
## Blouse
3 x white shirt with collar (long-sleeved/winter).
3 x white shirt with collar (short-sleeved/summer).
No sports shirts.
## Tie
Claret and grey with interwoven crest.

**Pullover**
Claret, V-necked. Fine-knit.
**Socks/tights**
Plain, no patterns.
**Blazer**
Claret, 100% wool. Embroidered
badge on left breast pocket.
**Shoes**
Black, low heel. No trainers.

For tap, you needed a black leotard
with sleeves no belt, thick black tights,
black socks and black tap shoes. The
black wrap-over cardigan was
'optional'.

For ballet, it was a white leotard,
sleeveless with belt, pink tights, pink
satin shoes with ribbons and black
leather shoes with elastic. The white
wrap-over cardigan was 'recommended'.

Then there was the character skirt:
black with three ribbons; the ballet
skirt: white voile; and the tap skirt:
black polyester.

For acting, three white T-shirts with
'Precious Gems' on the front and 'We
Sparkle Whatever the Occasion'
written on the back, plus black

tracksuit bottoms and black trainers.

Hair had to be tied back with scrunchies, black or white, depending on leotard colour, and school bags must be plain.

\*     \*     \*

Shortly after the list arrived, Topaz's mum started leaving the flat very early in the morning to clean an office in West Starbridge before the workers arrived, and came home late at night from cleaning an office in East Starbridge after the workers had left.

Topaz began to have bad dreams about turning up to ballet wearing a white leotard, black tights and trainers by mistake.

They bought the endless list of school uniform requirements, little by little, over the school holidays, but every time they went into the school outfitters and Topaz felt the plush claret-coloured blazer on the Precious Gems uniform list, her mother said it would have to wait 'until next week'. Eventually, they ran out of 'next

30

week's and the start of school was only days away. Then *disastrophe* struck.

*       *       *

A 'disastrophe' was the worst possible level on Topaz's three-level disaster scale. The 3D-scale took into account not only the actual nature of the disaster, but its context and potential consequences.

A minor annoyance was classed as a 'disasterette'. A major problem was upgraded to a 'disaster'. The worst possible disaster in the worst possible context with catastrophic consequences for life became a 'disastrophe'.

Take a broken nail.

A straightforward broken nail—if you weren't growing them—wouldn't feature on the 3D-scale. No one could be *that* shallow. Well, they could, but it was best not to acknowledge it. If, however, you *had* been growing your nails, a broken nail would be a disasterette.

31

If, on the other hand, you had spent weeks growing your nails, faithfully rubbing in cuticle cream every night, filing them to the same length and even using a pencil instead of your fingers to use the phone, a broken nail would be a disaster.

Suppose you had been doing all those things because you had a part in a television commercial as the hand of Velvet Glove hand cream. Because of your broken nail you couldn't do the commercial. A top director, who would have spotted you on the television, noticed your understudy instead. She then landed the lead role in the soap he was casting and you missed your one and only lucky break because of a broken nail. This would be a full scale disastrophe.

Disastrophes came in many forms and this one appeared in the shape of a second-hand maroon blazer hanging in the hall.

'Whose is the blazer?' Topaz asked when she saw it.

32

'Yours,' said her mother. 'I mentioned to Mrs Bostock-Brown, one of the ladies I clean for, how expensive blazers are. She thought you might like an old one her son Daniel has grown out of.'

'I can't turn up on the first day wearing a boy's blazer!' stormed Topaz. 'It's not even the right colour! I'll be a laughing stock! A moron in maroon! You simply don't understand!' Tears rolled down her face.

Topaz's mother wrung her hands as she looked at her sobbing daughter. It wasn't that she didn't understand; she did, but there was nothing she could do about it.

# Chapter Three

The start of school after the long summer holidays is always tinged with a mixture of anticipation and apprehension and the thought that time is no longer your own, but belongs to teachers and timetables. It is especially difficult if you are still suffering from the fallout of a major disastrophe.

\*          \*          \*

Topaz stood miserably at the bus stop

in the blazer that was wrong in every way. Her mum had sewn the Precious Gems crest on the blazer breast pocket, but the badge from Daniel's school had been bigger so you could see where the old badge had been unstitched and the new one sewn on. It made it seem as if the Precious Gems badge was surrounded by a halo.

*I might as well have 'freak' branded on my forehead*, she thought sourly.

When she had been at Starbridge Middle, mornings at the bus stop were usually fun—in fact, they were the best part of the day. Everyone met up, and, safely out of the sight of parents and snitching older brothers and sisters, rolled up their waistbands to shorten their skirts, turned up the collars of their shirts and blazers and replaced 'sensible' shoes with trainers. This morning, Topaz stood alone. She had to get two buses going west instead of one bus going east, so not only was she earlier than her friends, she was on the other side of the road, on her own.

For old times' sake she rolled up her waistband, but her blazer was so long it looked like she wasn't wearing a skirt at all. There was 'short' and *'short'*, but so short it looked like you were out in a boy's blazer and knickers was a fashion *faux pas* in anyone's stylebook.

*      *      *

First days of first terms at new schools always felt differently from any other days, but first days of first terms at stage schools *smelt* differently too. It wasn't just the smell of new uniforms, school bags and stationery, it was the scent of new musical instruments in their cases, bags of powdery white resin to stop the dancers from slipping, new leather tap-shoes and boxes of greasepaint.

Topaz stood in the corridor, looking as lost as she felt. She'd been given a key to her locker but she had no idea where her locker was.

In a room to her left she could hear people stuffing things into their lockers and banging the metal doors shut, giggling and chattering as if they had been at Precious Gems all their lives.

She felt a tap on her shoulder.

'New pupil?'

A pretty Oriental girl with glossy black hair pulled back into a high ponytail was standing behind her.

Topaz nodded. She felt pathetically grateful that someone had taken notice of her.

The girl beamed a megawatt smile. 'Hi! I'm Pearl Wong and I'm a senior pupil. I'll be looking after all the new pupils for the next few days. You might recognize me from the Speedy Snax commercial. It's running on TV at the moment.'

Topaz didn't but was obviously expected to. She gave Pearl a look which she hoped said, 'I know just the one.'

'I'm the girl eating the burger?' Pearl prompted. 'I didn't actually eat one because they're gross, but I had to act as if I was eating one.'

Topaz had thought there were several girls in the Speedy Snax commercial but didn't like to say.

As if reading her mind Pearl added,

'I'm the only one with a speaking part. I say M*mmm.*'

Topaz had never met anyone who had been in a TV commercial and the older girl saw the look of admiration on her face.

'*And* I said my line in one take. The advertising agency was thrilled with my performance!'

The corridor was filling up with excited pupils and Topaz began to feel bewildered by the newness of it all.

'Come on, let's get you to your locker before assembly,' said Pearl.

Topaz's heart sank. She'd have to walk into the locker room with all the chattering girls. The gossiping would stop as they stared at her.

'Are you in the right school?' one of them would sneer, looking at her blazer.

*Oh well, here goes,* she thought, slinging a bag over each shoulder.

Pearl continued to march ahead. 'First-year lockers are upstairs,' she shouted over her shoulder. 'Downstairs lockers are for senior pupils.'

A bell sounded and a tide of claret blazers and a single maroon one surged towards the school hall, the site of the auditions.

It was instantly apparent that pupils at Precious Gems viewed school assembly as a performance. Just by their posture you could tell who did what. The dancers stood up straight with their toes pointed outwards. The musicians couldn't help but conduct the music. The singers sang every song as if it were a solo. And the actors never followed any of the assembly, as they were trying to remember lines they should have learnt the night before.

Miss Adelaide Diamond, founder and Headmistress of the school, seemed to fill the stage, with her flowing clothes and rows of beads around her neck. She welcomed back the old pupils, welcomed in the new and ran through the staff changes since last term.

Topaz had tried to hang back because of the hateful blazer, so was wedged in at the back next to a weedy-looking boy with very long eyelashes who introduced himself as Jasper Pretty, and who kept cracking his knuckles.

Topaz couldn't help but notice that no one at the school introduced themselves with just a simple 'Hi!' or 'Hello!' An introduction was an opportunity to deliver their full name as a performance and make an impression.

Topaz practised in her head. 'Hi! I'm Topaz L'Amour.'

Yes, it sounded good. In fact it sounded *very* good.

\*       \*       \*

Last in meant first out of assembly, and Topaz came out of the hall and into the corridor to be met by Pearl, holding a clipboard.

'Hi!' she said to Pearl. 'I'm Topaz L'Amour.'

Pearl nodded. 'Yes, we've met, but now I can tick you off my list!'

Whilst they waited for the others Topaz said, 'I can't believe how short that assembly was. Ours used to drone on for hours.'

Pearl was looking over the heads of the pupils coming out of the hall and ambushing all the lost-looking ones with a cheery, 'Hi! I'm Pearl Wong,' and ticking names off a list.

'The less time in assembly, the more time to sing and dance!' she said, pulling another bewildered newcomer to one side.

About twenty new pupils had soon gathered around Pearl as if they were chicks milling around a mother hen. No one wanted to leave her side in case they got lost.

Topaz noticed Sapphire Stratton standing alone, a little away from the main group. She gave Sapphire a shy smile and Sapphire smiled back in an 'I'm lost too' sort of way.

Hearing a giggle, Topaz turned to see a group of girls behind her, nudging and whispering to each other. They were looking in her direction and obviously poking fun at her blazer.

*Stuck up cows!* she thought, glaring back at the sniggering crowd.

She marched over to Sapphire. 'Hi! I'm Topaz L'Amour. I sat next to you at the auditions.'

Sapphire seemed really pleased to see a friendly face. 'Hello, I'm Sapphire Stratton,' she said, adding slightly wistfully, 'but you probably know that already. *They* obviously do.'

She nodded in the direction of the group near her who were doing a very poor job of trying to point and stare without being noticed.

Topaz hadn't for one moment thought they were pointing and whispering about Sapphire. She'd been convinced they were laughing at her foul blazer. She let out a sigh of relief and giggled.

Sapphire looked puzzled.

'I thought they were all whispering and bitching about my blazer but they were whispering and bitching about you!' Topaz said, then wished she hadn't.

'Whatever's wrong with your blazer,' Sapphire said, peering at the maroon monstrosity, 'at least you can take it off. I'm stuck being a Stratton and I can't even introduce myself because everyone already knows who I am!'

Topaz *wanted* everyone to know who she was and couldn't understand why Sapphire didn't. She'd love to be famous and have a well-known name. Pointing and whispering and nudging were to be encouraged, if it was for the right reasons.

'Don't you like being famous?' asked Topaz.

'I just want to fit in,' Sapphire said sadly. 'To fit in you can't stand out. You have to be ordinary.'

# Chapter Four

Stage school was absolutely nothing
like Topaz had imagined, at least not
when you were a first-year with
practically no experience of anything
other than playing the third spear
carrier from the left in the Starbridge
Middle after-school stage club end-of-
term show.

She went through the first couple of
days in a muddle, forever running
through corridors between lessons,
finding she was on the first floor when
she should have been on the second, or

turning up with her ballet things when it was a tap-dancing class.

For the first two days there were no real lessons, only theatre classes so that pupils could be graded. Everyone did exactly the same classes, regardless of their musical, acting or dancing ability. One of the senior students would show them a dance routine or a mime, and the class had to follow.

Miss Diamond, Anton Graphite and Gloria Gold sat watching the classes and making notes.

Topaz had no idea how well she had done in mime. How did you know whether you made a convincing egg, boiling in a pan of water? She thought she held her own in the acting class, but singing and dancing were a problem. She did her best to keep up, but it soon became obvious that hours spent singing into her hairbrush or tap-dancing on the bathroom floor with drawing-pins in her trainers wasn't proper training.

In fact, she cringed when she remembered her singing class.

Up and down the scales they sang

until Miss Gold shouted, 'Hold at the peak!'

The high note seemed to go on for ever as Miss Gold walked along the row, listening to each pupil in turn.

Topaz began to feel dizzy. It was no good, she'd have to breathe. She took a huge gulp of air at the very moment that Miss Gold stopped in front of her and listened.

'I looked like a fish gasping for air,' she moaned to Sapphire when they were stuffing their things back into the locker at the end of the second day. Since they'd met the previous morning they'd been together all the time. Despite her perfect hair and being born with all the right connections, Sapphire wasn't the least bit stuck-up.

'They'll teach you how to breathe properly,' said Sapphire. 'Otherwise, during a long speech, you'll end up panting like a dog on a hot day.'

Pearl Wong bounded into the locker room. 'Everyone getting along OK?' she asked.

'Who are *they*?' asked Topaz, pointing towards the stream of people walking past the door. There were as many different ages, shapes, sizes and school uniforms as there were pupils.

Pearl had been very friendly all day, but for the first time, she wrinkled her nose as if a bad smell had suddenly wafted past. 'Those,' she said haughtily, 'are the PTs.'

'The PTs?' queried Topaz.

'The part-timers,' said Pearl in a voice that implied, Surely you've heard of the PTs? 'They come in after school for classes. What a bunch of duds! You don't have to be talented or anything. Just pay the fees. Miss Diamond would allow an elephant to join a PT ballet class if it could find a pair of ballet shoes big enough.'

The pupils giggled. How tragic to be considered a dud! What was Miss Diamond thinking, allowing these amateurs through the doors of

Precious Gems?

Topaz shuddered. She'd have to make sure she stayed well away from the PTs.

*      *      *

The third day at school held several shocks for Topaz.

Normal lessons began on the morning of the third day, and during the afternoon each new pupil had an appointment with Miss Diamond so they could be given their timetable for the term.

The first shock was that most lessons seemed to be the same as they would have been at Starbridge High. The thought that she was still doing so many of the same lessons as Janice Stone and Kylie Slate was almost too much for Topaz to bear. It wasn't that she hadn't realized she would have to do *some* of the same lessons as in a normal school. She just hadn't realized she would have to do quite so many and just how ordinary they would be.

She'd assumed that the lessons would

be delivered as a performance. Instead of the dry old maths teacher standing in front of her, droning on, she'd rather imagined the teacher bursting into class in a top hat and tails, singing a witty ditty about equations or fractions, and that the whole class would sing out the answer and repeat the verse as a chorus.

Some of the teachers actually seemed to resent the fact that the twenty or so faces sitting in front of them couldn't wait to get out of the classroom and on to the stage.

'I don't suppose that any of you really want to be here,' said the science teacher, Trudi Tuffstone. '*You* think you are all going to be stars. I've taught for years in front of classes of pupils who were convinced they didn't need an education. They were *sure* they were going to become famous. These pupils do appear in public,' she curled her lips in a smirk and gave a dramatic pause, 'but not on television. On the supermarket checkout at The Bargain Basket!'

'Miserable old toad,' Topaz said to

Sapphire as they left the class. 'She'd just love it if we all ended up waiting at tables or stuck behind a till.'

'She's right, of course,' said Sapphire.

Topaz looked horrified. 'How can you agree with her? We're here to be stars, not to learn about mating fruit flies or the life cycle of a broad bean.'

'I like science,' said Sapphire. 'I think I'd rather go to university and be a doctor than a star.'

\*     \*     \*

All the first-years were in the same class for academic lessons, but because everyone had such differing abilities when it came to performing, at two o'clock the class split up and everyone went their separate ways, sometimes into mixed-year classes. A first-former who was trained in ballet might find herself at the barre next to a third-former who until stage school had never even attempted a *plié* and was still struggling to catch up.

Until Topaz had seen Miss Diamond that afternoon, she had no idea what classes she would be in.

*       *       *

Topaz knocked on the door of Miss Diamond's office.

A crisp, clear voice called out, 'Come in!'

Miss Diamond had her head down and was making notes at her desk. She looked up briefly.

'Ah, Topaz. Take a seat. I'll be with you in a moment.'

Topaz looked around for a chair to sit on but there didn't seem to be the sort of chairs pupils should sit on, so she stood and looked round the room.

At Starbridge Middle the Headmaster's office was almost entirely grey. The wood-effect plastic desk was grey. The bookcases were grey plastic, the chairs were grey plastic, even the view out of the window was the grey tarmac of the playground. The only thing grey about Miss Diamond's office was her hair, which was the colour and consistency

51

of wire wool.

Her office was exactly as Topaz had imagined a star's dressing room would be, even down to the wall-mirror surrounded by lights. There were piles of cushions heaped on huge sofas, covered in the same plush red velvet as the curtains in the school hall. It was difficult to tell what colour the walls were as every inch was covered with framed posters of plays and films featuring Miss Diamond. Some of the posters showed her looking so young it seemed impossible to believe that the beautiful woman usually pictured in the arms of a handsome man was their Miss Diamond.

There were yellowing newspaper articles with headlines such as 'Diamond Does it Again!' and 'Diamond Proves a Precious Gem!' Stretching the length of the wall behind Miss Diamond's desk was a large glass cabinet full of awards and trophies.

Topaz was sure that some of them were Golden Nuggets but she didn't dare step any closer to get a better look.

Just as Topaz was beginning to wonder whether her mum might let her wire up twelve light bulbs around her bedroom mirror, Miss Diamond got up from her desk and beckoned Topaz to sit on one of the velvet sofas whilst she lowered herself on to the other.

The sofa may have looked comfortable, but instead of sinking into velvet delight, Topaz found it thin and lumpy. She could feel springs going *ping!* under her bottom the moment she sat down. She remembered the audition and her numb bum. Did meeting Miss Diamond always have to include torture for her bottom?

Even though Miss Diamond was ancient, Topaz could see that she had once been a very attractive woman. Everything about her, from the way she sat on the sofa, propped up by cushions, to how she folded her hands in her lap, screamed elegance.

Topaz tried to put her hands in her lap in the same way but noticed her elbows stuck out as if she was about to start doing an impression of a bird flapping its wings. She tried to fold in her winged elbows but this just made her hands look like flippers. In the end, she did what she always did when she was uncomfortable, and sat on her hands.

In trying to sort out her elbows, Topaz hadn't realized that Miss Diamond had been talking to her and was now offering her a piece of paper.

'Topaz?' said Miss Diamond, holding the piece of paper in mid-air.

Topaz pulled out her hands from under her thighs and took the piece of paper. There seemed to be an awful lot of classes listed on it.

'So, as I was saying,' Miss Diamond continued, 'I hope you won't feel too badly this term. We're very flexible and people do make astonishing progress. Starting this way in the first term doesn't mean it will have to continue like that. Really, it's down to you. We can provide the classes, only you can provide the commitment and determination. It will be hard work, but I'm confident that . . .'

Topaz had been staring at the typed sheet. It must have been given to her by mistake.

'I think there has been some mistake, Miss Diamond,' she said, trying to hand back the sheet. 'This has classes after school and on Saturdays.'

Miss Diamond's hands remained folded in her lap.

'That is what I have been saying,' she said. 'All of your fellow classmates have already had formal training in most of the theatrical disciplines. You have a great deal of potential, Topaz, but if you are to catch up to entry level, you will have to join the after-school classes with the PTs.'

# Chapter Five

From behind a row of coats hanging above a bench in the locker room came the sound of sobbing. There was no sign of a body, just sobbing interspersed with the occasional snort.

'Are you ill?' asked a voice. 'There's a school nurse.'

The sobbing got louder. It was as if the crying coats were enjoying having an audience.

'I'll go and get someone and they can ring your parents.'

There was a strange squeaking sound

followed by a gentle thump.

*Squeak-ker-thump. Squeak-ker-thump.*

Topaz poked her head round from behind the coats and saw a rather large girl with a broken leg and thick red plaits rapidly heading off down the corridor on a pair of crutches.

'Hang on!' Topaz shouted after her, rubbing her face on a nearby coat. 'I'll be OK.'

The girl turned and headed back towards Topaz. For someone on crutches she was amazingly speedy. Standing in front of Topaz, hanging over her crutches, she pulled out a cotton handkerchief from a bag slung across her shoulders.

'Here,' she said. 'Snot and stardom don't go together.'

Topaz blew her nose. She'd never used a proper hankie before, only paper tissues, and she wasn't sure whether you were supposed to hand it back full of bogeys.

The girl seemed to know what she

was thinking. 'Keep it,' she said. 'My mum packed my case with loads of clean ones.'

Topaz dabbed her nose and swung her legs over the side of the bench. 'Why doesn't she let you use tissues like everyone else?' she snivelled.

The girl rolled her eyes. 'She likes to do laundry. She's into that whole ironing knickers scene too. She once ironed a crease into the front of my brother's rugby shorts!'

The girls looked at each other in horror. Some mothers just had *no* idea.

'Does your mum pack your bag every morning?' asked Topaz, who had barely seen her mum over the last few days.

The girl shook her head.

'I live miles away and it was too far for me to come by bus every day, especially,' she waggled her broken leg in the air, 'with this thing. I'm boarding in the East Wing.'

Topaz had read about girls who went to boarding-school, but she had never actually met one and hadn't realized that you could live at Precious Gems.

'Mum wanted to drive me every day, of course,' the girl continued, 'but then she said in order to cope with driving into town, she'd have to take tablets to calm herself down, and Dad said that cars, tablets and Mum don't mix so there was a *huge* row, and Dad said I'd have to board during the week.'

'What about home?' Topaz asked her. She wasn't sure she'd want to be a boarder. The first few days had been so awful she'd been glad to get back to the safety of her tiny bedroom in Andromeda Road.

'I think Mum found the first night without me pretty scary,' said the redhead, completely missing what Topaz had meant. 'She rang me about twenty times to make sure I was OK. She only rang tcn times last night so I think she's coping a little better. Dad says it will do us all good for me to board.'

Topaz had stopped snivelling but was still feeling sorry for herself. Nothing about stage school had come up to her expectations and she was only halfway through the third day. Was it too late to start at Starbridge High? She was sure if she went there Janice Stone wouldn't go round with Kylie Slate any longer. Her mum wouldn't be happy about the uniform of course, but perhaps she could do a deal with her so that she didn't get any Christmas or birthday presents ever again instead. She was *that* desperate.

'Are you OK now?' the redhead asked.

Topaz shrugged. 'Yes and no.'

'Why the no?' She handed Topaz one crutch and, using the other as a lever, shuffled round and perched on the bench beside her. Topaz noticed that her plaster was completely clean. There wasn't a single mark on it. When Kylie Slate had broken her arm, running after the boys while playing Kiss Chase, *her* plaster had been covered in rude limericks.

Topaz's bottom lip wobbled and the tears started to flow again.

'I'm behind in lots of dance classes so I've got to join the PTs,' she said.

'Life's just one disastrophe after another.'

Topaz had fully expected heaps of sympathy from the redhead, but instead she said, 'I think it's good that the school takes people who can pay, even if they can't dance. That way, the school makes lots of money and can give people who can't pay a scholarship.'

Topaz looked up sharply. *She* was on a scholarship. So without knowing it she was already linked with the PTs. Why couldn't life be simple?

The two girls had been chatting away for ages, but they had forgotten to introduce themselves.

Topaz looked at her watch. There was probably a class she was supposed to be in, though she couldn't remember what.

'Thanks for the hankie. I'm Topaz L'Amour, by the way,' she said.

The redhead beamed. She had a very round and very friendly face. 'I'm Ruby,' she said. 'Ruby Ruddle.'

*       *       *

Sapphire Stratton had not been the only pupil to arouse curiosity at the start of term. The name 'Ruby Ruddle' had also been on everyone's lips.

Ruby was the pianist who had fallen off the stage into the orchestra pit at the auditions. Rumour had it that not only had she broken her leg in three places and smashed the conductor's podium on the way down, but she had sustained a rather unfortunate injury when she landed on an upright clarinet.

Although Topaz remembered someone falling off the stage at the auditions, she'd been too nervous to pay any attention or remember much about it, so when she asked Ruby why she was on crutches, Ruby had to explain from the start.

'I love playing the piano and the violin, I just get so terrified performing in front of an audience. I seem to lose the use of my legs. When I got up from the piano stool my legs just went to jelly, which is why I fell off the stage. That's one of the reasons Dad sent me here. He thought it might boost my confidence. *I* think the only solution is to put me in a harness and parachute me straight on to the piano stool.

'So, because it was an unusual break, they had to let the leg heal and break it again under anaesthetic, which is why I'm still on crutches. My plaster comes off in a week and *then* I'll be in trouble.'

Topaz looked puzzled.

'Mum said no one could write on the plaster. She thinks it's unhygienic. Just wait till she sees this!'

In a flash, Ruby yanked her skirt up to her waist to reveal a large pair of navy knickers, below which her plaster cast was covered with graffiti. Topaz took a closer look. Some of the things people had written were *very* rude.

'And what about . . . you know . . . the clarinet?' asked Topaz, who was dying to know if the rumours were true.

'What clarinet?' replied Ruby looking genuinely puzzled.

'They said, you know, you fell on a clarinet.' Topaz didn't want to spell it out.

Ruby shook her head. 'Oh, that's just a rumour. There was no clarinet. It was an oboe.'

# Chapter Six

Gradually, the days at Precious Gems
assumed some sort of routine, and
Topaz, though still not entirely happy,
began to settle in to life at stage
school.

Adelaide Diamond was determined
that her pupils would not only have
first-class training in the performing
arts, but would also hold their own in
academic subjects.

In order to fit in such a full
timetable, school started at eight-
fifteen with a ten-minute assembly,

and lessons began at eight-thirty precisely. Mornings and early afternoons were spent in academic lessons and then at two o'clock, everyone scattered to their various classes. Officially school finished at four-thirty, but most people stayed behind to rehearse plays or run through lines, or, if you were Topaz, join catch-up classes with the PTs.

Although Topaz had been horrified at the thought of going to classes with the PTs, she quickly found that the others in her class might not have had much talent, but they loved performing. The older students, who took the lessons in return for free tuition, usually made the sessions fun. Toes were stood on while tap-dancing, eardrums were pierced while singing, and arms and legs got entangled during ballet, all to fits of giggles and tears of laughter. Topaz thought of Anton Graphite's stony face when any of the full-time pupils so much as put a foot wrong in one of his dance classes and was grateful that she could practise her dancing without him.

*　　　*　　　*

The days were very long. Sometimes Topaz felt so tired she could barely bend her legs to do another *plié* and the noise of twenty people learning to tap-dance sent shockwaves through her head. She had felt like a star singing into her hairbrush and making up dance routines to songs on the radio. Now, she just felt as if everyone was better than her and no matter how many classes she did with the PTs, she would never catch up with the others.

*There must be a quicker way to stardom*, she thought as she took off her ballet-shoes and put on her tap-shoes. *Somehow, I've* got *to get noticed.*

*　　　*　　　*

The tight timetable and large number of different classes for differing abilities meant there was very little time to make friends. Weeks into the school term, there were several people in Topaz's class that she had never

67

really spoken to. She spent any free time she had with Sapphire, who didn't seem to want to go home, and Ruby, who was living in what the school rather grandly called the East Wing, but was really just a modern extension stuck on the back of the school. Because Ruby was a full-time boarder at the school, she had a key to the junior common room and thus, more importantly, access to a television.

It was lounging on the lumpy sofa in the common room one afternoon that Topaz had an idea. 'Quick!' she yelled, 'I need a pen and paper!'

Sapphire rummaged in her bag but only managed to find a lip pencil, which she tossed towards Topaz as Ruby rushed to grab some paper from her room.

A smooth voice flowed from the television as Topaz yanked up her shirt sleeve and began to scribble on her arm.

'*Proof of the Pudding* is looking for new contestants to join us for the next series. If you'd like to join Wendy Whisk in the studio, send your name, that of your cooking companion and your address to: *Proof of the Pudding*, Pulsar Television, PO Box 1422, Starbridge STAR YOU.'

In her excitement, Topaz had written down everything the announcer had said, so the message started at her wrist, went past her elbow and ended at the top of her arm.

'I love that programme,' said Ruby, who had come back in with enough paper to write a novel. 'Wendy is so funny and I love trying out the puds.'

'My mum met Wendy Whisk on a chat show and said she was a total cow,' said Sapphire.

Ruby ignored her. 'Why do you want the details anyway?' she asked Topaz.

Topaz gave a sly grin. 'I'm going to apply to be a contestant,' she said, sticking her arm out in front of Ruby who began to transfer the details on to a piece of paper.

'Are you a good cook?' asked Sapphire, to whom cooking was a total mystery. Nanny Bean didn't let her lift so much as a teaspoon and she'd never seen her mother do anything in the kitchen except open bottles of champagne.

Topaz shook her head, remembering the time she'd put a whole egg in the microwave. There'd been a massive explosion and the oven had taken for ever to clean. After that, her mum usually just left her something to heat up.

'I don't really even like cooking,' she said.

'Then why are you are going to apply to go on a cookery programme?' asked Ruby, struggling to get Topaz to stand still so that she could get the details off her arm.

'To get on television!' said Topaz. 'I can't hang around waiting to be a star. I've got to find a way to be noticed!'

Sapphire and Ruby gave a good-natured groan. Topaz was always announcing she was going to be a star.

'Do you honestly think that some big Starbridge producer or top agent is going to be watching *Proof of the Pudding*?' asked Ruby.

Topaz shrugged her shoulders. 'You never know. Sapphi, wasn't your uncle offered the leading role in *The Wild Escape* when he was standing in a chip shop?'

'That's true,' Sapphire said, nodding.

'Because,' said Ruby, exasperated, 'he went in with the producer to buy himself a battered sausage and a pickled gherkin.'

'It was a pasty and a pickled egg,' corrected Sapphire.

Topaz was undeterred. 'It's worth a try!'

'You'll have to ask Miss Diamond for permission first,' said Sapphire. The school was very strict on their pupils not appearing in public without its consent. 'You know you'll be in trouble if you don't.'

\*          \*          \*

After watching the post every day for what seemed like weeks, Topaz had heard nothing from the game show and had almost forgotten she had ever applied to be a contestant. So when at the end of assembly, Adelaide Diamond cleared her throat and said in an irritated voice, 'Would Topaz L'Amour and Ruby Ruddle report to my office immediately?' at first, she couldn't think what Miss Diamond wanted to see her about.

A red-faced Ruby caught up with Topaz as they streamed out of the hall. 'Why do you think Miss Diamond wants to see us?' she asked, noticing a flicker of fear cross Topaz's face.

'I've got no idea,' said Topaz brightly, though her stomach was churning and her legs felt like jelly. She had just remembered about the letter to the game show.

Miss Diamond's door was slightly ajar when the girls arrived.

'You knock!' whispered Topaz, pushing Ruby forward.

'No, you!' hissed Ruby, thinking that it was the only time Topaz didn't want to make an entrance.

'ENTER,' boomed a voice so loudly it startled the girls, and they almost fell through the door into Miss Diamond's study.

Instead of sitting at her desk or on one of the red velvet sofas, Miss Diamond was standing, her arms folded across her huge bosom, which looked as if it might break free from whatever undergarments kept it in place. The seniors had warned the juniors that the size of the swell of Miss Diamond's chest was directly proportional to the trouble you were in, and, since the beads around her neck were being tossed about like an inflatable dinghy in heavy seas, this was not a good sign.

Miss Diamond's chest gave an extra large heave. 'I received a letter yesterday.'

Topaz and Ruby waited for the dramatic pause before Miss Diamond continued her speech.

'It was from an old friend of mine. Petunia Bluff. Do you know her?'

She turned her back to the girls and stared out of the window. As the only view was the back of the school boiler room, they knew this was all part of

73

the performance. In spite of being worried, Topaz couldn't help but marvel at just how good an actress Miss Diamond was. No wonder she had won so many Golden Nuggets.

The girls had never heard of Petunia Bluff. 'No, Miss Diamond!' they said in unison.

'She's a TV producer at Pulsar Television. Are you sure you've never heard of her?'

'Yes, Miss Diamond!' said Ruby, noticing that Topaz hadn't said the same thing, and that she was now tracing a pattern on the threadbare carpet with her toe. A pink flush was creeping up her neck and on to her face.

Miss Diamond spun round, and, as if pulling a rabbit out of a hat with a flourish, brandished a letter. 'Then why are you writing to her?' she demanded.

Topaz bit her lip and continued to look down at her feet. By now her face was burning.

Miss Diamond handed Ruby the letter and asked her to read it out loud. Ruby instantly recognized Topaz's large looping handwriting from all the times she'd seen her practising her autograph.

She began to speak, but her mouth was so dry and the lump in her throat so large, all that came out was a high-pitched squeak. It reminded her of the time she'd let her hamster out of the cage for a run round the kitchen floor, just as her mother had come in through the door and stepped on it.

Dear Producer,

Ruby Ruddle and I are pupils at Precious Gems Stage School. We are both brilliant cooks and think your show is totally fab. Can we be on it?

Lots of love, Topaz L'Am♥ur xx

P.S. Miss Diamond, our Headmistress, is fine about all this, so no need to check with her.

Topaz didn't dare look at Ruby and Ruby couldn't bear to look at Topaz.

Miss Diamond was now sitting behind her desk, her arms folded over her ample chest. The beads seemed to have stopped quivering. She leaned back in her chair. 'Luckily, Petunia thought to check with me before contacting you. Topaz, I *know* you are eager to fast forward your life and become famous, but Ruby, I am surprised you were part of this. You all know the school rules about performing in public without permission.'

Ruby could feel hot tears pricking her eyes. Topaz was still staring at the carpet and noticed a tear splash on to Ruby's shoes. It was all too much. She couldn't let poor Ruby take any of the blame. Now was the time to give a performance worthy of a Golden Nugget.

Remembering her breathing lessons, she took a deep breath, lifted her head and said, 'Miss Diamond. It is all my fault. Completely. Utterly. Totally. In my selfish desire to appear on television I involved Ruby in a deception of which she had no prior knowledge.'

Miss Diamond and Ruby stared at Topaz, who was beginning to enjoy herself.

'In my defence, I would like to say that my intentions were honourable though my methods were questionable and—'

'Enough!' said Miss Diamond, raising her hand, whilst at the same time thinking what a good performance Topaz was giving.

'Topaz, you are in my office, not in a court of law, but I understand the point you are trying to make. It is to Ruby's credit that she did not immediately blame you and to yours that you admitted you were entirely responsible for the letter. Let's leave it at that.'

Topaz couldn't believe she'd got off so lightly. Surely there would be some kind of punishment? But Miss Diamond was letting her leave.

As Topaz reached out to grasp the

door handle, Miss Diamond called out, 'Ruby, you can go, but Topaz—we're not finished yet.'

*I knew it!* thought Topaz turning back. *It was just too good to be true!*

Miss Diamond was holding out a sheet of paper. 'Filming starts a week today. I will take you in the minibus. We'll leave here at three-fifteen to be there at three-thirty. Filming is live at four-thirty.'

\*       \*       \*

When Topaz emerged from Miss Diamond's office, Sapphire was trying to console Ruby, who was still upset. From the look on Sapphire's face, Ruby had obviously told her what had happened.

'How *could* you?' asked Ruby as they walked away from Miss Diamond's office. 'You *promised* you'd ask Miss Diamond first.'

'I'm sorry, Rubes,' said Topaz sheepishly. 'I really didn't think that we'd be chosen—and I didn't think Miss D would let us go anyway.'

78

A look of panic swept across Ruby's face. She'd fully expected Miss Diamond to tell Topaz that they couldn't go on the programme. Now it seemed she was going to have to face television cameras and an audience.

'But why me? Why not Sapphi?' she asked desperately. 'You know I get stage fright!'

Topaz had forgotten. She shot Sapphire a look which said, 'Help me!'

'Don't look at me,' laughed Sapphire. 'I've never even used a microwave. This is your mess.'

'It'll be fine,' said Topaz, in a voice that sounded far more confident than she felt.

# Chapter Seven

To try and say sorry for upsetting Ruby, Topaz promised that as soon as they all had some free time, she'd treat them to a four-cheese toastie at Happy Al's Café, which was round the corner from the school. Luckily for Topaz, the opportunity came later that day, when the senior pupil due to take the after-school singing class swallowed a fish bone at lunch, and was told by Starbridge General Hospital not to speak for a few days.

When the girls pushed open the door

of Happy Al's Café, they were surprised to find they were the only ones there. Row upon row of tables covered with plastic red-and-white checked tablecloths stood empty. There wasn't even the usual smell of cooked breakfasts that hung in the air all day.

'Where is everyone?' asked Sapphire looking around. 'I can't even see Happy Al.'

\*　　　\*　　　\*

Happy Al was the most miserable person the girls had ever met.

Having spent years playing non-speaking parts in soap operas and TV commercials, he'd been thrilled to be cast in the starring role of Inspector Barry 'Nosey' Parker in the prime-time crime investigation show, *Murder Mile*.

His first words were, 'It takes twenty years' experience to know that man has been murdered,' spoken whilst standing over the body of an actor with a fake knife sticking out of his chest.

Those few words thrust Al into the

limelight in a way he had only dreamed of. He was so happy. He couldn't believe his good luck.

'Al! Al!' people would shout out as he drove through Starbridge in his bright red open-topped sports car. He could walk straight to the front of the queue outside The Super Nova nightclub and the bouncers on the door would immediately unclip the velvet ropes and usher him through. Inside, drinks would be on the house and pretty girls would flutter their eyelashes at him. There was always a table reserved for him at Starbridge's top restaurant, The Truffle Pig, at which he would discreetly dine with a succession of rising young starlets.

Not discreetly enough to avoid the gossip column in *The Starbridge Gazette*, however. Eventually, his long-suffering wife, Norma, got fed up of reading over her cornflakes about what her husband was up to and moved abroad, taking most of Al's money with her.

After being in the show for a few years, Al started to notice that people thought he really *was* Nosey Parker. They didn't seem to know him as Al.

On a chat show the host kept calling him Nosey. 'So, Nosey, what are your future plans?' the host asked.

'It's Al,' he would correct with a forced smile.

The man in his local paper shop greeted him every morning with a cheery, 'Solved any murders today, Nosey?'

Even the autograph hunters didn't want his real name. 'Could you write "Nosey Parker"?' said one lady, pushing a pen and paper towards him, 'or my son won't know who you are.'

Al began to get anxious about being typecast. He hadn't been to drama school to spend all his life pretending to be a policeman. If he'd wanted to spend his life as a policeman he'd have become a real one.

He rang his agent, Zelma Flint. Her assistant put the call straight through.

Zelma soothed his worries.

'Al, honey, the world's your oyster. My phone's hot with offers of work for you. If you gave up Nosey tomorrow, work would pour in. Trust me, I'm your agent!'

When *Murder Mile* was moved from its prime-time Saturday night slot to late night on a Monday, Al became worried.

'Should I be worried?' he asked Zelma, when he finally managed to get her on the phone at the third time of trying.

'Honey, you're an institution,' she rasped. 'Nosey Parker will be on our screens for years.'

But then *The Starbridge Gazette* ran an article claiming that *International Speed Tiddlywinks*, shown on another channel at the same time, was getting twice the viewing figures of *Murder Mile*.

He rang Zelma Flint. Her assistant said, 'Miss Flint is unavailable to take your call.'

Al called Zelma five times and five times her assistant said exactly the same words.

Six months before his contract was due for renewal, Al was summoned to the offices of Pulsar Television for a meeting with 'management'.

Usually when he walked through the door there was a bottle of his favourite tipple on the desk, a box of fat cigars and a thick silver pen to sign his new contract. This time the desk was bare. The chair behind the desk was facing the window and all he could see was a pair of elbows sticking out each side. The chair never moved, but every so often a puff of thick cigar smoke would billow out like a smoke signal.

'So sorry,' said the elbows. 'It's time for Nosey Parker to hang up his handcuffs. We're ending the series immediately and not renewing your contract.'

'But . . .' began Al.

The elbows twitched and another puff of smoke rose into the air. 'There's no one left to arrest. Everyone is either dead or you've put them in prison already. Close the door on your way out and remember to hand in your car-park pass.'

Al trudged out. In his dressing room, someone had already packed fifteen years of his life into a cardboard box. A brass plaque with his name rested on the top. It had fallen off the door some time ago but no one from the maintenance department had thought to replace it.

Al looked at the plaque.

*Did it fall or was it pulled?* he thought, picking up his box of belongings and leaving his dressing room for the last time.

Al never spoke to Zelma again. Occasionally, her assistant would phone and ask him if he wanted to open a supermarket, and there was once an opportunity to play a laughing policeman in a pantomime, but Al had had enough of show business.

'I'll never work in this town again,'

he vowed.

Of course he did, but this time behind the counter of the café he opened a year after the series was axed.

*      *      *

Al appeared from the kitchen and leaned across the counter. 'Yes?' he grunted.

'Where is everyone?' Topaz asked him.

Al shrugged his shoulders. He looked even more miserable than usual. 'Speedy Snax are killing my trade,' he said, angrily flicking the counter with a tea towel. 'They've just opened another branch down the road. You seen the TV ads?'

The girls nodded. Pearl Wong told anyone who would listen that they were re-running her ad, this time with a voice-over at the end saying, 'Now in West Starbridge!'

'It *is* quiet,' said Topaz. 'Can't you do an advert, too, and then we could be in it?'

'Do you girls think I'm made of money?' he said bitterly, continuing to take out his anger on the tea towel. 'Speedy Snax is massive. It's got over three hundred and fifty branches across the country and hundreds of employees. Happy Al's is just me. I can't even afford to hire a waitress, let alone pay for a commercial.'

No one knew what to say. Whatever they said, it wasn't going to get rid of competition from Speedy Snax.

Topaz felt sorry for Al but she had other things on her mind.

'We've got problems too!' she told him. 'Ruby and me are contestants on *Proof of the Pudding* and we can't think what to cook!'

Al threw the tea towel over his shoulder and thought for a moment. 'Chocolate mousse,' he said. 'It's easy and everyone loves it.'

'I don't suppose you have a recipe?' asked Topaz hopefully.

'No, I don't!' snapped Al. 'Are you girls going to order?'

'We'd like three four-cheese toasties, please,' she said.

Al grunted. 'They're off the menu.'

'How can you have a café that doesn't serve a toasted-cheese sandwich?' asked Ruby, who had been looking forward to her toastie.

'You didn't ask for a toasted-cheese sandwich,' Al growled. 'You asked for a four-cheese toasted sandwich. I can only afford to buy one sort of cheese, not four.'

When Al brought over the one-type-of-cheese toasties, underneath the plates was a neatly written recipe for chocolate mousse.

'Thanks, Al!' chorused the girls.

'Humph,' said Al, disappearing into the kitchen.

*       *       *

For the next week, Ruby spent every evening in the tiny kitchen in thc East Wing perfecting the chocolate mousse recipe. Every morning, she'd put a container of quivering chocolate mousse before her classmates.

On the first day they all agreed it was delicious and asked for another spoonful. On the second day, no one asked for seconds. By the third day everyone said, 'Just a tiny spoonful' and by the fourth no one wanted to see chocolate mousse ever again.

'Don't you think you've practised enough, Ruby?' said Sapphire as she forced down another spoonful. 'It's all delicious.'

Ruby furrowed her brow. 'I can't decide whether to use milk chocolate, dark chocolate or a mixture of both,' she said. 'That's the mixed version. Topaz, what do you think?'

The cooking part of the cookery programme didn't interest Topaz in the slightest. She'd bring a bought pudding and pass it off as her own if it was a chance to be on television.

'I don't mind,' she said.

'What about white chocolate?' asked Ruby.

'Ruby, I don't care!' said Topaz, a little more sharply than she meant to.

Ruby, though usually good-natured, was getting more and more nervous as the day of the filming approached, and hadn't forgotten that it was Topaz who had volunteered her for the programme in the first place.

Ruby exploded. '*You* were the one who wanted to go on this show and you've shown absolutely no interest in my chocolate mousse whatsoever!'

'Steady on, Rubes,' said Sapphire. 'It's only a daft game show.'

Even Topaz was surprised at Ruby's outburst. 'Don't worry, Ruby, all you have to do is cook whilst I entertain the audience. You love cooking, I love being centre of attention. What could possibly go wrong?'

# Chapter Eight

A sign had gone up on the school notice-board, announcing that Topaz and Ruby would be contestants on *Proof of the Pudding* and if any of the other pupils would like to support the school and be in the audience, they should sign the list. The thought of getting out of lessons, even theatrical ones, to go to a TV studio was so exciting the list had grown longer and longer. Eventually, it was decided to cancel all classes after three o'clock so that everyone from Precious Gems could go, as long as they wore their T-shirts with Precious Gems written across the front.

Much to everyone's relief, there were so many names on the list there was no way everyone was going to fit into the minibus, so the school had to hire a coach instead.

Miss Diamond was the world's worst driver, and on several occasions, pupils had turned up at auditions so traumatized by the journey, they had been either white with fear or green with travel sickness. It didn't help that the outside of the minibus said: 'Pupils of Precious Gems Sparkle Whatever the Occasion', so that even when they felt as if breakfast was going to make a surprise reappearance, Miss Diamond would tell them to look out of the windows and smile.

'However you feel, the show *must* go on,' she would bellow, shooting round another corner on two wheels.

\*        \*        \*

A Starbridge Starliner coach pulled

into the car park of Pulsar Television, and as the pupils clambered down the steps they were met at the bottom by a man shouting, 'Audience to the left, contestants to the right.'

Before they knew it, Ruby and Topaz had been separated from the main group, and were being ushered along a corridor by a nervous-looking girl carrying a clipboard and wearing a T-shirt which said 'Pudding' across the front and 'Staff' on the back.

'Here we are,' said the nervy girl, opening a door marked *Green Room*. 'A few things to remember. Don't speak to Miss Whisk until she speaks to you. If you give me your ingredients I'll put them on the table. Always stand on the cross marked on the floor, oh, and please, please, never *ever* use the line "the Proof of the Pudding".'

'Why?' asked Topaz.

Nervy girl looked even nervier and backed towards the door. 'Because,' she said in a horrified voice, 'it's Miss Whisk's show. You are just the contestants.'

The girl tossed them a couple of aprons.

'You are the Spice team, the others are Sugar. Good luck!'

Topaz could hardly tie her apron she was so excited. 'I can't wait to meet Wendy Whisk. I wonder what the other contestants are like?'

Ruby was nervously muttering to herself, 'Melt the chocolate, whip the cream, grease the mould . . .'

\*      \*      \*

Moments later, the door flew open and, as if blown in by a hurricane, a very small, thin woman burst into the room.

She spoke in a series of rapid gasps, and hardly looked at Ruby or Topaz. 'Hi. I'm Wendy Whisk. Welcome. Nice to meet you.'

Wendy looked nothing like she did on television. Her blonde curls were stiff with hairspray and her face was so caked in make-up it looked as if someone had used an icing bag to pipe on her features. She had long, dangly earrings. Topaz noticed they were a miniature fork in one ear and a knife in the other.

'I'm sure you know the rules,' said Wendy Whisk, her head bobbing around so much her earrings whirred like helicopter blades. 'Just remember, guests are to be seen and not heard unless spoken to, and I am in charge.'

And with that, she left.

Ruby was disappointed. The woman they had just met seemed nothing like the warm, friendly Wendy they were used to seeing on television. Perhaps Sapphire's mother was right after all?

Topaz was starting to feel as nervous as Ruby. Wendy Whisk had made it quite clear that *she* was the star and that her guests were only there to make her look good. But star quality would always shine, she reminded herself, and if she only had Wendy to worry about, it would be fine.

Down the corridor came the sound of several sets of heels rapidly approaching the Green Room.

A shrill voice shrieked, 'I hope we're not late.'

The voice sounded horribly familiar.

'We've got heaps and heaps of people in the audience.'

Topaz felt her stomach lurch. It couldn't be, not here, not today, not now!

The heels were rapidly advancing on the Green Room and the voice was getting louder and louder.

'Have we mucked things up for you? That would be so totally like me!' the voice shrilled.

'No problem,' they heard the nervy girl say. 'There's still time for me to introduce you to the other contestants.'

Topaz gulped. Ruby, who had been nervously chewing the end of one of her plaits, saw her friend go pale and stopped in mid-chew.

*Please*, thought Topaz. *Please let it be anyone other than . . .*

The door swung open and the nervy girl announced, 'Topaz, Ruby, meet Octavia Quaver and Melody Sharp. They are from Rhapsody's Theatre Academy and they are the Sugar team!'

Topaz glared at Octavia. They hadn't

met since Octavia had stolen Topaz's number at the audition. She must have been offered a place at Rhapsody's. There was intense competition between the two stage schools. Whereas at Precious Gems it was acknowledged that everyone had different abilities and personalities, girls from Rhapsody's were all of the same type. Loud, brash and *very* confident. Monster stage-school brats who thought they were the bee's knees. It was rumoured that Rhapsody girls would stop at *nothing* to get a part, and the two schools were bitter rivals.

The nervy girl saw Topaz recognize Octavia and said brightly, 'So you already know each other? How super!'

'Oh yes,' said Topaz sourly. 'We know each other.'

Octavia looked blank and said with a sneer, 'Do we?'

Topaz seethed with fury. She'd spent *months* fuming over the way Octavia had double-crossed her at the audition, and Octavia didn't even remember her!

'You stole my number at the audition. Remember?'

Octavia shrugged. 'Vaguely,' she said, looking bored.

All four girls stood silently in the Green Room fiddling with the strings of their aprons. Eventually, Topaz couldn't bear it any longer.

'So, Precious Gems didn't offer you a place, then?' she said.

Octavia glared. 'I *chose* to go to Rhapsody's Theatre Academy,' she snarled. 'It's much more *me*. Pupils from there get *loads* of jobs, don't they, Melody?'

'They do,' said Melody, nodding.

Topaz didn't know whether that was true or not. Until she'd gone to Precious Gems she'd never even heard of Rhapsody's Theatre Academy.

Octavia sniffed and looked around the room. 'I'm very familiar with TV studios, of course.'

'Are you?' said Topaz, who could have kicked herself for sounding interested in anything Octavia had to say.

'Oh yes,' Octavia replied. 'I've been in front of a camera since I was six weeks old. As a baby I was the face of Grubbs' Gripe Water. Wasn't I, Melody?'

'She was,' said Melody.

Octavia smoothed her apron and said in a smug voice, 'My mum made sure I worked all the time. Adverts, knitting pattern covers, packs of nappies, I've done them all.'

'She has,' said Melody.

'And of course I got the part in the commercial for Slurp 'n' Burp fizzy drinks.'

'I haven't seen the commercial,' said Topaz, through gritted teeth. 'Perhaps your face didn't fit after all.'

Octavia gave Topaz a withering look and tossed her hair. 'Of *course* my face didn't fit! It was a radio commercial. The producer said the timing of my burps was superb.'

'Your mum must be very proud,'

Topaz said to a smirking Octavia, 'having a daughter who can burp along to music!'

Ruby giggled, Melody tried to stifle a smile and Octavia looked stung.

The door of the Green Room opened and the nervy girl popped her head round.

'So glad you're all getting on,' she beamed. 'Are you ready?'

Octavia moved forward.

'Come on, Mel!' she barked over her shoulder.

Pushing past Topaz she hissed, 'Don't try and get smart with me. You'll *never* win.'

# Chapter Nine

Topaz squinted into the bright lights and looked around. The studio was much smaller than she had imagined. She hoped her mum had remembered to set the video recorder to tape the show.

A voice from the gallery above the studio rang out over a tannoy. 'The redhead on Spice. Can you get her to take her shades off?'

Topaz turned round to see Ruby was wearing sunglasses.

'Take them off!' hissed Topaz.

'I can't,' whispered Ruby. 'These are my usual glasses. The lenses have turned dark because of the lights.'

Topaz had forgotten that because Ruby needed to wear glasses all the time, she had special lenses that turned dark in bright light. It meant she didn't have to carry a separate pair of sunglasses around.

The floor manager looked perplexed. 'Don't you have any ordinary glasses with you?' he asked.

Ruby shook her head.

It wasn't only the floor manager who wanted Ruby to ditch the dark glasses. 'You'll have to take them off,' said Topaz, worried that Ruby would begin to look the mysterious star. Only stars wore sunglasses indoors, and if anyone on their team was going to look starry, it had to be her.

'I won't be able to see!' said Ruby.

'Don't let a little thing like that worry you,' Topaz said as she whipped off

103

her friend's glasses and handed them to an increasingly anxious-looking floor manager.

'Positions please,' boomed the voice over the tannoy.

Octavia and Melody made their way to the left-hand side of the studio and Topaz headed off to the right.

'Could the Spice redhead move into position?' boomed the tannoy.

Topaz turned to see Ruby rooted to the spot.

'What now?' hissed Topaz as she went back to get her friend. 'Are you so nervous you've lost the use of your legs?'

'No,' said Ruby. 'I'm just blind now I haven't got my glasses! I don't know which direction I'm heading in.'

Topaz steered Ruby to the Spice kitchen area.

'Everyone ready?' crackled the tannoy.

A wiry man suddenly jumped out on to the floor of the studio and shouted, 'Lights, Camera, *Action!*' and the theme music for *Proof of the Pudding* blared out.

As the music faded, Wendy Whisk bounded on to the set to a cheering audience.

'Hello, and welcome to another episode of *Proof of the Pudding*.' Wendy threw her hands up in the direction of the audience who shouted back, 'Is in the eating!'

Topaz noticed that at the same time, a girl stood by the camera and held up a huge sign saying, 'Is in the eating'.

'We've got an extra-special show for you today. Watch closely, because you could be looking at the stars of the future!'

The placard girl held up another sign which said, 'Clap'.

The audience did as they were told.

'Both teams are from stage schools right here in Starbridge. So there are two questions today. Who will be the future star, who will be the winners, and will that be the same team?'

*That's three questions*, thought Topaz, who was finding Wendy Whisk very irritating already.

Wendy bounded across to Topaz and Ruby. 'And who do we have on the Spice team?' she shrilled, her earrings whirring around her neck.

Topaz smiled into the camera and purred, 'I'm Topaz L'Amour and this is Ruby Ruddle. We're both pupils at Precious Gems Stage School in Starbridge.'

Topaz flashed another smile whilst Ruby looked like a rabbit caught in car headlights.

'So Topaz, what will you and Ruby be cooking for us today?'

'Today, Wendy, we'll be making chocolate mousse.'

'And?' said Wendy, who was obviously expecting Topaz to say something else.

'And,' said Topaz, 'it will be delicious.'

Wendy bounded over to the Sugar team. 'And who do we have here?'

'I'm Octavia Quaver and this is Melody Sharp. We're both pupils at

Rhapsody's Theatre Academy in Starbridge.' Octavia smiled sweetly.

*Phoney*, thought Topaz.

'How wonderful!' gushed Wendy. 'And what will you be cooking for us today?'

'Well, Wendy,' said Octavia, 'today we'll be cooking a sumptuous peach and raspberry meringue cake filled with fresh cream and accompanied by a light mixed-fruit coulis.'

Topaz was mortified. Octavia's recipe sounded delicious. How could Happy Al have let them go on the show with just chocolate mousse?

After a few more comments about stars of tomorrow and cooks of today, Wendy raised her golden whisk and announced, 'Let the cooking commence.'

Octavia and Melody immediately got to work, stirring and whisking and tasting and pouring.

Topaz and Ruby stood surrounded by implements and ingredients, but did nothing.

After a few moments and when the camera was on the hateful Rhapsody girls, Topaz whispered to Ruby, 'Why aren't you cooking?'

'I can't even see the ingredients, let alone see to cook them,' hissed Ruby, fumbling on the counter. 'You'll have to get my glasses back.'

But the glasses were in the back pocket of the highly-strung floor manager, who was darting in and out of the shadows at the edge of the studio.

Topaz tried a little wave to attract his attention, but caught the eye of Wendy Whisk instead.

'How's it going, girls?' she asked, looking at the unopened ingredients.

'Just fine,' said Topaz with a forced smile.

'The others seem to be working away,' said Wendy, looking puzzled.

Topaz glanced over at Octavia who smirked back. 'We take a relaxed view of cooking,' Topaz said, biting off a corner of the chocolate and getting foil wedged between her teeth.

'And where did you get the recipe?' asked Wendy, wondering what on earth was going on.

'Happy Al, the owner of Happy Al's Café in West Starbridge, gave it to us,' said Topaz.

'Jolly good,' said Wendy, in a get-on-with-it tone of voice.

After Wendy had leapt back to the smirking Sugars, Ruby muttered to Topaz, 'I can remember the instructions, just do what I tell you.'

But by this time, Topaz was in a complete state. Octavia's meringues were already in the oven and the light fruit thingy was whirring in the blender. Only half-listening to Ruby's instructions, Topaz smashed up the chocolate with a rolling pin and bunged it into a saucepan to melt. Eggs were cracked and cream went flying. Every ingredient on the counter was put in a bowl and stirred frantically. Finally, Topaz threw the gloopy chocolate mixture into a mould, just as Ruby said, 'And then it needs at least ten minutes in the fridge.'

A gong sounded. Wendy raised her golden whisk and shouted, 'Teams, stop cooking!'

The girls stood surrounded by a

sticky mess. Topaz was covered in chocolate and cream and eggs and sugar. Bits of chocolate mousse hung off her eyebrows and stuck to her hair. Ruby stood squinting into space, unaware that she too was covered in chocolate mousse.

Octavia and Melody looked as fresh as the moment they walked in. Even their aprons were spotless.

Wendy called both teams over to a table. Topaz picked up the mousse and put out a sticky hand to lead Ruby over, but Ruby wouldn't move.

'Oh, come on!' hissed Topaz wearily. 'The worst is over.'

'My shoe is stuck to the floor!' said Ruby, almost in tears as she kicked off her shoes.

Topaz squelched across to the table and Ruby padded across in stockinged feet. Octavia and Melody danced over as if they had wings.

'Remind us again of what you cooked and how you cooked it!' said Wendy as Octavia placed her spectacular dessert on the table.

Whilst Octavia ran through the

recipe, Melody cut small slices and handed them around the audience.

'Mmm,' said the audience who clearly thought it was delicious.

Octavia shot Topaz a smug grin.

'I think we know how much the audience liked that!' crowed Wendy.

Turning to the dishevelled Topaz and Ruby, Wendy asked, 'Tell us again what you cooked and how you cooked it!'

'It's Happy Al's chocolate mousse and I just bunged everything in,' said Topaz, scowling at Octavia.

Watching the television in his café, Al put his head in his hands. 'If only she didn't keep mentioning my name!' he groaned. 'I just seem to attract failure!'

Topaz began to turn out the chocolate mousse from its mould. There was a plopping sound, and the camera zoomed in on what seemed to resemble a large dark brown cow-pat on a plate.

'And this is Happy Al's recipe?'

111

asked Wendy, looking horrified.

'Yes!' said Ruby brightly, unaware of the state of the plate in front of her.

In his café, Al put his head in his hands and wailed, 'I'm ruined!' Then looking around his already empty café, wailed, 'I'm doubly ruined!'

With sticky hands, Topaz spooned small portions of the chocolate cow-pat on to paper plates, and passed them around the audience who stared at the brown mess in front of them.

Suddenly Sapphire's voice rang out. 'This is a totally fab pud. Try it.'

As the audience gingerly tasted the brown goo, a murmur went round the studio. 'Oooooh', 'Yummmm' and 'Delicious'.

Wendy Whisk's eyebrows shot up so far they disappeared under her hairline. She grabbed a spoon and began to tuck in to the remainder of the mousse.

'I say, this really *is* heavenly,' she said smacking her lips. 'Is this really chocolate mousse?'

Topaz suddenly realized that all was not lost. Octavia's scowling face told her that.

Topaz pretended to giggle. 'Silly me! Did I say chocolate mousse? I must have been nervous. The recipe is called Chocolate Mess!'

'Well, it's fabulous!' said Wendy, her eyes rolling with pleasure as she licked the plate.

Happy Al raised his head from where it had been slumped on the table. '*Please* mention my name again!' he pleaded towards the TV.

'So,' said Wendy, her face covered in chocolate. 'Audience—which is it to be? The Sugar team's meringue thingy or Happy Al's heavenly Chocolate Mess from the Spice team?'

The audience held up their signs. It was unanimous. Topaz and Ruby had won!

'Yes!' shouted Al at the TV.

'A surprise winner!' announced a breathless Wendy, as she handed the Spice team their prize, a plastic whisk sprayed gold and mounted on a

113

block of wood.

Topaz saw Octavia sobbing in the corner and Melody trying to console her.

Topaz beamed and thrust the trophy in the air triumphantly.

'Ours may not have looked the most attractive but . . .' she paused dramatically and brushed her hair out of her eyes, smearing more chocolate on her face, 'I always thought we'd win.'

Topaz turned to face the audience. 'However good something looks on the surface, the proof of the pudding,' she threw up her hands in the direction of the audience who roared with her: 'is in the eating.'

Wendy Whisk turned a violent shade of red, her lips pursed and her earrings whirred manically.

*      *      *

Meanwhile, in downtown Starbridge in a tiny office stuffed with dog-eared scripts, agent Zelma Flint had been watching *Proof of the Pudding* out of the corner of one eye.

She jabbed the intercom button on her telephone.

'Get me Adelaide Diamond,' she barked at her assistant. 'That Topaz girl is interesting.'

# Chapter Ten

Adelaide Diamond had thought the success of Topaz's appearance on *Proof of the Pudding* might have gone to her head. It was one of the reasons she hadn't told Topaz that the agent Zelma Flint had been trying to get in touch with her.

Several of the older students had reported to her that Topaz was working hard and got to classes on time, even the difficult-to-get-out-of-bed-on-Saturday-morning type of classes. Not only that, but she proved to be a fast learner.

Adelaide had asked Anton Graphite to pop in, unannounced, on one of the after-school tap classes, and although it had obviously almost choked him to admit it, even he had been surprised at how quickly Topaz was moving ahead.

'But she's still got a long way to go,' he huffed.

Gloria Gold had also been surprised at Topaz's progress. She had worked very hard in the breath-control classes, and whilst some of the other students were still going blue in the face and forgetting to breathe in the middle of a long speech or song, Topaz seemed to know instantly what was required.

'I *am* surprised, Adelaide, I don't mind admitting it,' she said, sucking air through her teeth and making a whistling sound. 'She's made rapid progress, but the question is, for how long?'

\*        \*        \*

Topaz sat on one of the big velvet sofas in Miss Diamond's office, and,

117

remembering how thin and lumpy they were, also sat on an overstuffed cushion which said, 'Actresses do it to Applause'. This was a mistake; she felt as if she was perched on a pedestal and could topple over at any moment.

At Starbridge Middle you only ever went to the headmaster's office for a telling-off. She didn't know why Miss Diamond had asked to see her this time but she couldn't think what she could have done wrong. The explosion in the chemistry lab hadn't been her fault, even though she had weighed out the ingredients for the demonstration. Whoever had typed up the instruction sheet had put grams instead of micrograms. Even the science teacher had admitted that Topaz wasn't to blame. She said she didn't mind about her fingernails; she was sure they'd grow back.

\*          \*          \*

'How do you feel you are getting on, Topaz?' asked Miss Diamond.

Topaz wobbled on the cushion on

the sofa. She should have put up with the pinging springs. 'Sometimes I think I'm doing OK, and other times I feel like a worm.'

Miss Diamond smiled. 'A worm?'

Topaz nodded. 'You've never seen a worm tap-dance or do ballet or heard it sing scales, have you?'

Miss Diamond had to admit that, in her long career, she had never come across a performing worm.

'That's because they can't!' exclaimed Topaz. 'They're genetically unable to tap-dance!'

Adelaide Diamond thought she might explode with laughter, but she wasn't a five-times winner of a Golden Nugget for nothing. Her face could portray one emotion whilst experiencing quite another.

'What I think you are saying,' she said to the forlorn-looking girl in front of her, 'is that you feel you don't have it in you to do all the things you want.'

119

Topaz nodded and the cushion shook. 'I thought I would be performing by now. I'm just so not into schoolwork and I don't seem to be any nearer to being a star.'

Adelaide Diamond had suspected this might be the case. She'd given the girl a hard workload in the first term and she had more than taken up the challenge. Topaz's performance on *Proof of the Pudding* had given her a taste of stardom. She didn't want her to become despondent now. If she was to continue to work this hard she would need a little encouragement.

'How would you like a small part in the Christmas show at the Theatre Royal?' she asked Topaz, who instantly toppled off her cushion with shock.

\*         \*         \*

'Oh, that's brilliant. Well done you!' said Sapphire, when Topaz tore into the locker rooms bursting with her news. 'You must be thrilled!'

'I am,' said Topaz, who had secretly been a little disappointed that she hadn't been inundated with offers from agents after her success on *Proof of the Pudding*. 'This could be the big break I've been waiting for!'

'What sort of part are you playing?' asked Sapphire.

Topaz shrugged. 'I don't know, but it's a chance to be on stage and get noticed, so whatever it is, it's got to be good.'

*　　　*　　　*

The Starbridge Christmas Show ran for one night only and wasn't even at Christmas; it was at the beginning of December. This was because it raised money for charities in and around Starbridge and all the performers appeared without getting a fee. Helping the needy of Starbridge was one thing, but not if it got in the way of several weeks' work in pantomime and a fat cheque.

In the past, the principal actor or actress could nominate their chosen charity to which all the box-office proceeds were donated. This was

changed after a bit of a rumpus when an actress had nominated the Hamster Rescue Society. *The Starbridge Gazette* had reported that whilst some children in the town didn't get any presents on Christmas Day, hamsters in Starbridge were eating grapes and running on top-of-the-range hamster wheels.

*     *     *

Sapphire and Ruby didn't seem to have any plans for Christmas. There was a Christmas concert at Precious Gems, but because so many pupils were busy with pantomimes or shows, this was smaller than the one at Topaz's old school. From what Topaz could gather, the Precious Gems end-of-term Christmas concert was really just a carol concert without many carols.

Ruby didn't mind in the least that she hadn't got a performance lined up for Christmas. Now that she was out of plaster and her leg was strong, she could use the pedals on the piano and had no excuse not to appear on stage.

She loved playing the piano, but still couldn't conquer her stage fright. Even the thought of walking on stage made her head swim and her heart race. Unless she came up through a trapdoor and left the same way, she didn't see how she was ever going to manage to be on stage without her wobbly legs giving way. It would be *so* embarrassing if, having just got rid of her plaster, she fell off the stage and broke her leg again.

*      *      *

Sapphire seemed a little quiet when Topaz asked her about her plans for Christmas. Topaz had been hoping to get a glimpse of Sapphire's mother because, other than Miss Diamond, she'd never seen a proper actress close

123

up. But whenever she broached the subject, Sapphire always changed it.

'What are you up to at Christmas?' she asked her.

Sapphire shrugged. 'I'm not sure,' she replied. 'It depends on whether my parents are in the country.'

\*　　　\*　　　\*

Sapphire hadn't heard from her mother since the start of term.

'How are the big cats?' Sapphire asked when her mother finally rang one evening from some exotic location where she was filming a television mini-series about living with lions.

It was the sort of mini-series where the viewer was expected to believe that despite trekking through a jungle all day in the sweltering heat, it was entirely possible to keep your hair and make-up immaculate.

'Oh, darling, I don't get near any lions,' her mother said. 'Think of the insurance if I got so much as a scratch! Is Nanny Bean looking after you?'

Sapphire cringed. She felt far too old to have a nanny, but Nanny Bean refused to let Sapphire call her anything else. 'I've powdered your backside and burped you. I'm not about to start letting you call me foreign names,' she had once said in front of Sapphire's friends when she'd tried to introduce her as 'Miss Bean the au pair'.

'Everything's fine,' Sapphire said. 'When are you coming home?'

'I've simply no idea, darling,' cooed her mother. 'The heat is playing havoc with my energy levels, so we are a teeny weeny bit behind with the filming schedule.'

Sapphire knew all about her mother's energy levels. It probably wasn't so much the heat that was causing her to lounge in her air-conditioned trailer all day, but the effects of too many champagne cocktails the night before.

'When is Daddy coming home?' Sapphire asked. 'Will *he* be home for Christmas?'

Her mother sighed as if this was the most tiresome question her daughter could have asked. 'Sweetie, you know he's touring. Directing this play is very important to him. Even *I* don't know where he is or when he'll be home.'

Sapphire felt tears pricking behind her eyes. It looked as if it would be another Christmas with just her and Nanny Bean. They wouldn't even have a proper turkey. Nanny Bean said it would be a waste because they couldn't get through the leftovers. Chewing cold turkey played havoc with her false teeth. 'If there's just the two of us I'll buy a lovely turkey meal for one from The Bargain Basket and do extra sprouts!' she'd say.

'Will *you* be home by Christmas?' Sapphire asked her mother.

There was a muffled sound at the end of the line. 'Sweetie, darling, I'm losing you, we're cracking up, I'm losing the line.'

The phone went dead.

Sapphire trudged upstairs to her bedroom, flopped on the bed and stared up at the ceiling. She knew her mother wouldn't ring back. Not once had she asked how she was getting on at school.

*I don't know why it upsets me*, Sapphire thought to herself, clenching her fists. *I should be used to it by now*.

She rolled over and buried her face in her pillow. If only her parents had asked her what she wanted, she'd have told them she wanted to go to an ordinary school and take ordinary exams, not a stage school. But they hadn't, and by the time she had plucked up the courage to tell them, they weren't around to tell.

# Chapter Eleven

Topaz was beside herself with excitement at the thought of appearing in the charity concert at the Theatre Royal in Starbridge. This could be her big break. As so many stars took part there was bound to be someone in the cast or in the audience who would spot her potential. A term at Precious Gems had convinced her that although she didn't have any experience, she did have lots of potential. Wasn't that what Miss Diamond had said? 'You have a great deal of potential, Topaz.'

'Potential,' she said to herself. How she loved that word.

There didn't seem to be any auditions and no one had told her what part she was to play, but whatever role it was, Miss Diamond had obviously immediately recognized that it was right for her and had recommended her to the theatre director. The only slight worry was that no one had told her anything about attending rehearsals.

'I would have thought,' said Ruby, chewing the end of one of her plaits, 'that if you were going to be involved in musical numbers you would be involved in the rehearsals. Even top musicians can't just turn up and perform.'

Sapphire agreed. When she was younger she'd spent plenty of time reading in the wings whilst her parents attended rehearsals.

'I think you'd better ask Miss Diamond for more details,' she said. 'Just think how awful it would be if you turned up on the first night and didn't have a clue what you were doing!'

*       *       *

Adelaide Diamond assured Topaz that there was no need to worry, that she would be accompanied to a rehearsal the day before the performance, and that she could wear her ordinary acting clothes, the black tracksuit bottoms and white T-shirt with the Precious Gems slogan across it.

'You'll be assisting the Great Hamboni with the magic tricks,' she said to Topaz, who almost fainted with delight. 'They'll give you a costume when you arrive.'

Topaz thought being a magician's assistant was the perfect role. She didn't need to prove she could act, dance or sing. She could just stand there, wearing sequins, and be a star. All those people who doubted her ability would have to eat their words when they saw her on stage.

Other than her mum, who was trying to rearrange her evening cleaning jobs, she wasn't sure who else to invite to the theatre. She thought about Janice

Stone, but after she had been snubbed in favour of Kylie Slate she decided against it. No, they could read about her in *Snapped!* and say, 'We used to know her.' Oh well, her mum would have to do.

*      *      *

'I'll be wearing masses of sequins, probably silver ones, and I'll do things like . . .' Topaz flung out her arm and pointed at the marmalade jar as if it had magically appeared on the table.

Topaz's mum was pleased that so early on at stage school her daughter seemed to have landed a starring role in the charity concert. It would have been better if she could have been paid—Christmas was coming up after all—but she could see how happy Topaz was. It was not often her daughter had smilcd during the past few months, and although they hadn't seen much of each other, she was concerned at how hard she was working.

*      *      *

Amidst the excitement of appearing on stage, Topaz began to worry that she might have to hold a rabbit pulled out of a hat. She'd once stroked a rabbit called Nibbles in the Children's Corner at the zoo, and after the zoo keeper had put a plaster on her bleeding finger, he'd said that Topaz was the first person Nibbles had ever bitten.

'Rabbits can tell if you don't like them,' he had said, shaking his head. 'If you don't like them, they'll let you know.'

Before being attacked by the ancient lop-ear she had liked rabbits, but now she hated them, and if they *could* tell, she was sure the magician's rabbit would savage her in front of the audience.

\*　　　\*　　　\*

Pearl, who occasionally acted as chaperone to the first years, had been given the task of accompanying Topaz to the rehearsal the day before the show. Some of the pupils were taken to auditions in the school minibus, but she and Pearl stood in the bus shelter on which was stuck a poster announcing:

**A Spectacular Event in Aid of Charity**
**The Theatre Royal Starbridge Presents**
**A Night of Magic and Music**

'I'm starring in that show!' Topaz wanted to shout at the others in the queue. 'I'm going to be wearing sequins and wrestling with ferocious rabbits!'

\*      \*      \*

Backstage, the theatre was a hive of activity. Topaz felt grateful that Pearl was there and seemed to know where to go and what to do.

Pearl pointed to a woman sitting behind a table handing out slips of paper. 'Queue up over there, give your name and they'll give you a number. I'll stand by this pillar and wait for you.'

Just as Topaz approached the table, she felt a sharp elbow in her back, pushing her to one side. A girl stood in front of her and flicked her long blonde hair over her shoulder, whipping Topaz on the cheek so hard it stung.

'There! *There!*' she was saying, jabbing her finger at the list. 'Make sure you tick me off. Now give me my number.'

Topaz was furious and tapped the girl on her shoulder. 'There *is* a queue. Can't you wait your turn like everyone else?'

The girl spun round, her hair hitting Topaz on the other cheek. It was none other than Octavia Quaver.

'Oh, get a life!' she snapped before

stalking off.

'Did you see that?' fumed Topaz as she went back to Pearl, clutching her numbered slip of paper. 'Who does Octavia Quaver think she is?'

'A Rhapsody girl?' asked Pearl.

Topaz nodded.

'Ignore her,' said Pearl. 'She's just typical of the sort that go there.'

\*       \*       \*

Topaz found herself standing in another line, yet again next to the poisonous Octavia Quaver. The two girls did their best to ignore each other.

A small man came rushing into the corridor clapping his hands furiously.

'Numbers 234 and 235 to the stage immediately,' he shouted, flitting up and down the row. '234 and 235 to the stage immediately!'

Topaz looked at her number. 235. She began to move towards the stage at the same time as Octavia Quaver who, it appeared, was number 234.

The last time Topaz had been on a

stage was at the auditions for Precious Gems, and that seemed ages ago. Then she'd thought the stage at the school theatre was the most wonderful place to be, but it was nothing compared to standing on the vast stage of the Theatre Royal in Starbridge.

The house lights were up so she could see the tiers of cherry-red velvet chairs in a gentle curve, stretching towards the back of the theatre. Golden boxes decorated with little cherubs hugged the walls and a huge crystal chandelier twinkled from the ceiling. The rows of footlights in front of her seemed to mark the point where reality ended and fantasy began.

\*      \*      \*

'So,' said the magician to Topaz and Octavia, 'all you have to do is get into the box when I tell you. I'll then close the doors, say the magic word *Abracadabra*—'

'Both of us in the box?' interrupted Topaz. She didn't fancy sharing her starring moment with anyone, especially not an evil Rhapsody girl.

Octavia Quaver clearly felt the same way about Topaz as Topaz did about her. 'Together?' she shrilled.

'Well, of course,' said the magician. 'When the door is closed, could one of you neigh and whinny a couple of times as you go down the steps so I know when I can open the door and show you have disappeared?'

'Neigh?' asked Topaz.

'Whinny?' said Octavia.

The Great Hamboni looked puzzled.

'Don't you know *anything* about the trick?' he asked.

Topaz and Octavia shook their heads.

The magician rolled his eyes in horror and let out a huge sigh. 'I can't believe no one has told you!' He pointed at Topaz. 'You're the back end of a pantomime horse. Your friend's at the front.'

# Chapter Twelve

'You're very quiet,' said Pearl as the bus rattled through the streets of downtown Starbridge on the way back to the school. 'Are you all right?'

Topaz bit her lip and continued to stare out of the window. It was bad enough playing the rear end of a pantomime horse, but to find yourself a backside behind the bum of spiteful Octavia Quaver was too much to bear, especially as she'd set her heart on wearing sequins. Tears began to well up in her eyes.

Pearl nudged her. 'Topaz, I said, are you all right?'

Topaz turned away from the window and shrugged her shoulders. 'I don't know,' she said to the older girl. 'Life just seems one disastrophe after another.'

Even though Pearl wasn't quite sure what a disastrophe was, Topaz's face told her it wasn't good.

'It's just not what I expected,' said Topaz, wiping her eyes on her blazer. She hadn't actually managed to tell Pearl what part she would be playing in the Starbridge Christmas show, as even saying the words 'horse's bottom' made her break out in a cold sweat. All she had said when Pearl had met her in the wings was that the part was 'very small'.

The part may have been small, but the horse had an enormous backside. Just in case the audience missed her vast rear end, there was a little string to pull every so often which flicked her tail.

'A part is only as good as you make it,' said Pearl, patting Topaz's arm.

139

'Think about my Speedy Snax commercial. I made it my own. Make this part your own.'

Topaz groaned inwardly. She liked Pearl. She'd been very kind to the first-years, but now they'd had almost a whole term of hearing about her commercial.

Pearl took out her bus pass and waved it at Topaz. 'When I first saw I had one line, I could have been disappointed. I could have approached the part like this . . .'

She looked blankly at the bus pass and said in a monotone, 'Mmm.'

'But I didn't, I thought the part through. The burger was actually cold and greasy, but I *imagined* it to be hot and yummy and so I went . . .'

She raised the bus pass to her mouth, looked at it lovingly and, rolling her eyes with pleasure, said, 'MMMMmmmmm!'

The woman in the seat in front turned round in astonishment and Topaz had an overwhelming urge to stick her tongue out. Pearl didn't seem to notice and was chattering on.

'The director said that I hadn't just felt the moment, I had *smelt* the moment and it showed. Use all your senses.'

Topaz remembered the smell of stale sweat in the costume, and, never a good traveller at the best of times, began to feel sick. Pearl was still re-living her moment.

'The burger was cold and greasy but I still—'

Topaz grabbed her bag and, reaching up to ring the bell, said to Pearl, 'I feel a bit sick. I'll walk the last stop.'

*      *      *

Topaz staggered out of the bus and slumped on to a seat in the bus shelter. She'd felt hot and sweaty in the bus, but the sharp cold air of the December afternoon gave her a slap in the face and she soon felt better. As she came out of the shelter she saw a swarm of grey heading towards her. In the fading light it was difficult to make out what it was. At first she thought it must be fog rolling in, but it was something much more terrifying. It was a group of Starbridge High girls walking towards the bus stop, eating chips. She knew they usually hunted in packs. If she hadn't gone to Precious Gems she would have been one of them.

Topaz put her head down and began to walk on.

'Well, if it isn't Little Miss Wannabe Famous,' said a voice which she recognized.

The sea of blazers parted and there, stuffing chips into her mouth, was Kylie Slate. Standing next to her was Janice Stone. Topaz noticed that it was actually Janice who was holding the chips and Kylie who was eating them. Janice looked like a waiter.

Topaz ignored Kylie and said to Janice, 'How's the High? Did you see me on *Proof of the Pudding*?'

From the look on Janice's face, it seemed she was about to answer, but then Kylie stuffed a chip into Janice's mouth.

'A crummy game show! Not been in any movies yet?' Kylie sneered. 'Not snogged anyone famous?'

Topaz could feel herself going red with embarrassment.

The group around Kylie sniggered. Topaz wondered if Janice would have done so, too, if her mouth hadn't been stuffed with chips.

'Actually,' said Topaz in a voice which she hoped sounded strong yet casual, 'I've got a part in the Starbridge Christmas Show tomorrow.'

'Oooooh,' chorused the group sarcastically.

'Really hit the big time, haven't you?' Kylie sneered.

Topaz had had just about enough of the day and wasn't going to let a bully like Kylie Slate boss her around. What was it Octavia had said?

'Oh, get a life, Slate, you slug,' she snapped.

\*     \*     \*

Topaz hung up her blazer in the locker room. It was covered in grease marks.

The Slate gang had pelted her with chips as she'd legged it from the bus stop. Thank goodness her mum had promised her a new one for Christmas.

Topaz began to get ready for her ballet class with the PTs. She'd imagined slipping into the class and saying casually, 'Sorry I'm late. I've just been to my rehearsal for the Starbridge Show.' At which point all the no-hoper PTs would cluster round and ask her what part she was playing, and she would just wave them away and say, 'Oh, just a little something which requires me to be *drenched* in sequins.'

Now there was no way that she wanted to be asked anything about the show.

As she held grimly on to the barre, Topaz wasn't listening to the swish of leather ballet shoes on the wooden floor or the voice of the teacher shouting, 'One and two and three and four . . .' She went through all the moves like a robot.

The PT girl in front of her had a *huge* bottom which jiggled up and down and left and right every time she moved. Topaz stared at it. If the girl had a tail she wouldn't even need a costume to play the back of a horse.

*I've been totally miscast*, she thought, as she went through another routine. *Why me?*

But then she remembered the conversation with Pearl. What was it she had said? 'Make the part your own.'

*That's it!* she thought. *I'll make my backside a backside to be remembered!*

# Chapter Thirteen

The Theatre Royal was humming when Topaz arrived. She felt much more confident now she had decided that being the back end of a horse was better than not being on stage at all, and that there might be a way of making her bottom stand out, so to speak.

Ruby and Sapphire were going to be in the audience, as well as her mum, who had managed to get someone to take over her evening cleaning jobs. Topaz felt a little guilty that she hadn't told anyone that she wouldn't be wearing sequins and pulling rabbits out of a hat, but she'd worry about that later. Her mum had even paid for her to have a proper wash and blow dry at the hairdresser's, as she knew how much Topaz loved having straight hair. But as she tossed her glossy mane in the mirror, all Topaz could think was, 'What a waste of a straight-hair-moment.'

\*　　\*　　\*

The nearer the time came to the start of the performance, the more manic everyone became. The Great Hamboni wasn't due on until just before the interval, so there was plenty of time for Topaz to look around.

She wandered into the wings and peered round the side of the stage. The auditorium was filling up fast and she could see Sapphire and Ruby sitting in the front row. She waved, but they were too busy eating sweets and studying the theatre programme.

The programme! She'd completely

forgotten about it. Any moment now they would see the words: Horse, back end . . . Topaz L'Amour.

She ran out of the wings and straight into a man who had been sweeping the stage.

'Please can I have a programme?' she asked him, untangling her legs from the broom. 'I need to see how they describe my bottom.'

The man pointed to a box of programmes in the corner. Topaz grabbed one and scanned the pages. There didn't seem to be any mention of her name. She couldn't decide whether to be pleased or not. Then she saw it, in tiny letters underneath the cast list as part of a long list of people mentioned in the 'Special Thanks' section.

THEATRE ROYAL STARBRIDGE

THE STARBRIDGE CHRISTMAS SHOW

Just seeing her name in print made everything seem worthwhile. The classes with the part-timers, losing her friend Janice Stone, the wall-to-wall lessons, the horrid blazer, even Octavia Quaver.

*I've arrived!* thought Topaz. *I've really arrived!*

*              *              *

The unmistakable squawk of a Rhapsody bird rang out as Octavia Quaver marched towards the wardrobe department flicking her long blonde hair.

'I've got heaps of people in the audience,' she was shrilling to no one in particular. 'Heaps and heaps.'

Topaz was already in costume and practising flicking her tail. It was quite

149

fun to flick her tail and wiggle her bottom every time a good-looking boy came past.

The wardrobe mistress handed Octavia the front end of the horse. It had a very mean face with a wild look in its eye.

*Perfect casting*, thought Topaz, flicking her tail again as a cute chorister walked past.

'Make sure you tie that hair back,' the wardrobe mistress said to Octavia. 'You've already got one mane on that horse, you don't need another.'

Octavia snorted. 'I'm not going to tie my hair back. Who's going to see it, anyway?'

The wardrobe mistress shrugged. 'On your horse's head be it!' she said.

\*     \*     \*

Bells had been ringing for the last half-hour with the stage manager calling down the performance over the loud speaker.

'Half-hour call.'

'Twenty-minute call.'

'Fifteen-minute call!'

'Ten minutes!'

With every announcement the atmosphere behind the scenes became more feverish.

The Great Hamboni came rushing up to them stuffing doves into his pockets. 'Do you girls know what you're doing?'

Topaz felt nervous. 'Could you just run through one more time?' she asked.

Octavia looked as if a bad smell had wafted under her nose. It had. One of the doves had objected to being pushed into a pocket, and the Great Hamboni was trying to rub a rather nasty green and white stain off his jacket with one of the coloured silk handkerchiefs stuffed up his sleeve.

He spoke rapidly. 'The horse comes on. I speak, blah-de-blah. I lead you into the box. I shut the door. I open the door. You're still there. I shut the door again. The trapdoor opens. When it opens you whinny or neigh and immediately go down the steps to the trapdoor. I then say the magic word, "Abracadabra". I open the door, you're below the stage. The audience thinks you've gone. They clap. When you hear the clapping come back up the steps on to the stage. Stand in the box. The trapdoor will close. When I say the words "Hocus pocus", neigh, I open the door and you'll be there. Audience will go wild. You will come out. Take a bow and go. Got it?'

Topaz's head was spinning, but she nodded as the Great Hamboni ran after an escaped dove.

*     *     *

A bell sounded and the theatre manager called over the intercom, 'Beginners to the stage. Beginners to the stage. Five minutes to curtain up. Five minutes.'

'Do you think we should have practised?' Topaz asked Octavia. 'We've never actually been up and down steps in the costume.'

'Oh, for goodness' sake,' Octavia snapped. 'All you have to do is follow me. How hard can it be?'

'And now, as the grand finale to my act, I'd like to introduce you to my friend the racehorse, Red Dobbin!'

Topaz felt an almighty push from behind, and, bent double, hidden under brown fake fur and clutching Octavia's waist, she trotted out on to the stage to stand in front of the Great Hamboni. The audience roared with laughter.

'Of course, Red Dobbin has seen better days!' bellowed the magician.

The audience laughed again. Topaz couldn't see a thing but she could hear Octavia making the odd snorting sound and feel her pretending to paw the ground with her hooves. Two could play at that game, she thought, pulling on the string and flicking hcr tail. Octavia snorted again so Topaz did a little dance and wiggled her bottom. In the audience, people were laughing and thinking, *That is the most uncoordinated pantomime horse we've ever seen!*

Octavia began to move forward to the horse box, but Topaz had been so busy flicking her tail and wiggling her bum she hadn't realized Octavia had started to move. The front end of the horse was becoming detached from the back! Topaz lunged forward, but instead of grabbing Octavia's waist, got a handful of long hair. Octavia shrieked and stamped the ground with her hooves. Topaz tried to find her waist again but got an even bigger handful of hair. There seemed to be far more hair than waist and in the dark she couldn't tell what she was grabbing. She could hear the audience laughing. Eventually she got hold of Octavia's waist.

'Just get in the ruddy box,' hissed the magician, leading the horse by its ears.

The box was closed, opened, and closed again. The trapdoor opened and Octavia yelled 'Neigh,' and clattered down the steps leaving Topaz trailing behind.

\*     \*     \*

It was very cramped under the stage and packed with low beams and machinery. Octavia-the-horse was standing with her hands on what would have been her hips.

'You deliberately yanked my hair, you cow,' she hissed, stamping her hooves.

'I'm a horse, not a cow,' snapped Topaz, 'and *you* should have tied your hair back.'

Octavia was livid. She was almost blowing steam out of her horsy nostrils. 'I couldn't move my head because of you! Do it once more,' she warned, 'and I'll get you!'

The two girls were lined up on the stairs waiting for the magic words, 'Hocus pocus'. Topaz dived down and went to grab Octavia's waist but got more hair.

'You . . .' Octavia tossed her head and began to swing round but misjudged the length of her nose, hit an overhead beam and fell off the stairs.

Topaz stared down at what appeared to be half a dead horse. *I've killed a pantomime horse!* she thought.

'Hocus pocus!' came the words from above.

The horse moaned and began to rub one of its hooves.

'I've hurt my ankle,' it said. 'I think I've broken it.'

'Hocus pocus!' shouted the magician.

The noise of Octavia howling in agony brought people rushing from all directions.

*'Hocus pocus!'* yelled the Great Hamboni.

*The show must go on!* thought Topaz, *and I must go on with it.*

She clambered up backwards into the horse box, pulling the trapdoor shut behind her. Sticking her bottom out and bending over as far as she could, she let out a loud high-pitched whinny.

A relieved Great Hamboni flung open the stable door to be greeted by a furiously swishing tail, surrounded by a pair of huge buttocks covered in brown fake fur.

The audience clapped enthusiastically. The horse swished its tail again and wiggled its bottom. The audience went wild and the back legs did a little curtsey before the Great Hamboni slammed the stable door shut and shouted, 'THE END!'

Topaz crouched in the box. She'd felt so at home on the stage as the sound of laughter and applause rang in her ears. There was no doubt in her mind she was going to become a star.

'This isn't the end,' she said to herself. 'This is just the beginning!'

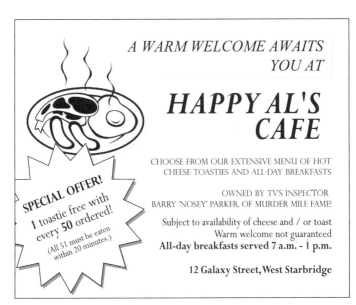